TWILIGHT'S ENCORE

WOUNDED HEARTS #3

JACQUIE BIGGAR

Cover Design and Interior format by The Killion Group
http://thekilliongroupinc.com

DEDICATION

I have so many people I'd like to thank. First, and foremost my husband, Robert John. Without you I wouldn't have had the courage to pursue my dreams, thank you.

My mom, who has always been my guiding light and allows me to toss ideas with her. Thank you.

To my daughter, Brandy, who is my inspiration.

To my critique buddies, you know who you are. Without you pushing me to better myself, this book might never have happened.

To my beta readers for their tremendous input, and the reviewers, who are key to a writer's success. Thank you.

And to Kim Killion and Jennifer Jakes, for the beautiful cover I'm so proud of, and the formatting and uploading services you provide. Thank you.

All the world's a stage
And all the men and women merely players;

William Shakespeare

CHAPTER ONE

Ty Garrett knew this day was going to suck the moment he opened his eyes. The sun streaming in through his half closed curtains told him what he'd already guessed. He was late for work. He groaned and rolled over, covering his face with a cool pillow. He owned the company, but still held himself to the same standards he expected from his employees, and going to work with a massive hangover was not his idea of normal.

Dressed in the only clean clothes he had left, Ty stumbled down the hall of his rancher style home in search of coffee. He threw in a pod of Italian roast, grateful for the fancy machine Aunt Tess had bought him for a house-warming gift. While waiting for the water to heat he grimaced around a jaw-cracking yawn and leaned against the butcher-block countertop to survey the changes he'd made to the seventies-style kitchen.

Even though it wasn't the main reason he'd bought the house, he liked the open plan design. A granite countertop separated the kitchen from the dining room with breakfast stools he'd lined up like little wooden soldiers. As soon as he moved in he'd replaced the avocado green appliances with state of the art stainless steel. A six burner stove with a built in barbecue flame broiler took pride of the place.

The hiss of the machine signaled that his thermal mug had finished filling. He scratched his flat belly and heaved a reluctant sigh. Time to face the music. It wasn't that he didn't love his job, he did. It was *this* job that was getting to him. *She* was getting to him.

Katy Fowler.

Just the thought of her name was enough to set his already iffy stomach swirling. Why she had to have some big fancy wedding here in Tidal Falls when she lived in LA was beyond him. She had to make all kinds of dough in her high falutin' career as a surgeon. She didn't need to come back here and rub it in his face.

He knew her decision to get married in her hometown had nothing to do with him, but that didn't make him any happier. She'd cut him out of her life a long time ago. Every bit as thoroughly as she cut into her patients chests.

Whatever he thought about their relationship, obviously it hadn't meant diddlysquat to her. Fine. Lesson learned. It just really sucked to find out she was now his client; at least until he got the Twilight Theatre finished. Then he planned on a lo-ong fishing trip. Far away. There was no way in hell he was going to be in town while she tied the knot with some other twerp. He wasn't a masochist. He'd only taken the job on because he couldn't stand to see that graceful old building fall to ruin.

Ty jammed a Yankee's ball cap on his head and grimaced at the pain. Why anyone ever got drunk when they had to wake up to this, he wasn't sure. Keeping a death-grip on his coffee he trudged out the door to his pick-up, only to come to a sliding stop on the asphalt drive. No truck. Great. He'd forgotten that Jared gave him a ride home in the wee hours from Duke's Bar. Now he really was going to be late. There was no sense calling the town's taxi service either. Hell, it would be faster to walk.

Ty cursed life in general and alcohol in particular and gritted his teeth against the brightness of the sun. Every step he took was accentuated by the pounding in his head. It was going to take him a good fifteen minutes to make it downtown. Well, she'd just have to twiddle her thumbs. There wasn't much he could do about it. The thought of having to see her this morning—after all these years—was the reason why he'd ended up drunk in the first place, so technically it was her own damn fault.

Just as he worked himself up to a good angry-at-the-world pace, Ty heard the sound of a diesel engine idling up behind him. He glanced over his shoulder to see Jared pulling up to the curb in a great black beast.

"So, how's the head?" A deep voice rumbled from within the cab.

"It's just ducky. Aren't you supposed to be at work?" If he remembered right, though admittedly things were pretty foggy at the moment, Jared had asked him for a job last night.

"Yeah, well. I was there bright and early, just like the boss-man said, but there wasn't anyone to tell me what to do, so I left."

"*I* can tell you what to do." Ty muttered, the noise of the truck reverberating inside his poor skull. "You here to give me a ride, or just chat it up?"

Jared had the audacity to laugh, before pulling a few feet ahead so Ty could climb gingerly inside. He was still trying to belt up when Jared punched the gas. The truck leapt forward, jerking him backward in his seat. Shooting Jared a fuck-off-and-die look Ty slowly raised his coffee to his lips, daring the asshole to try that again. Even best friends had their limits.

Jared grinned, his smile laced full of mischief. "Someone got out on the wrong side of the bed this morning. Or did you even make it to a bed?"

"Two words," Ty leaned his head against the cool glass and sighed with relief. "You're. Fired."

In response Jared reached over and turned up the volume on the radio to a screeching noise reminiscent of a close encounter with a fire siren.

And smiled.

The asshole.

Katy wandered around the interior of her family's old theatre reminiscing about the past when she should be attending to the hundred and one things on her list for today. The musty smell of rotted wood made her wrinkle her nose in disgust. She couldn't understand how her parents let the gorgeous old building fall into such disrepair. It was depressing and only highlighted the broken status within the Fowler family dynamics.

Her brother was gone off fighting someone else's war, who knows where, and her father had traveled halfway across the country chasing his youth with some woman just a few years older than she was herself. And then there was her mom.

Katy's mother gave a new term to the word perfectionist. Never a hair out of place or a crease in her thousand dollar power suits, she ran the board of directors at Katy's hospital with an iron fist. Her colleagues called her Foul Fowler behind her back, not that it mattered. She was what she was and made no apologies. Took pride in it, in fact. And that's what she wanted for her only daughter, power with a capital P.

It didn't matter what Katy wanted. It never had.

Shaking off the past, she peeked behind the big tan tarp blocking the main room from the entry, and gasped. It'd been completely torn apart. How did they plan to have this restored in the month and a half that was left before her wedding day? Katy's father had hired the company for the job, saying over the phone it was the least he could do since he couldn't make it home until the week before the wedding. She hoped he'd done some research before hiring whoever this was, because at the moment it looked as if he'd been scammed. The owner of the company couldn't even be counted on to be on time for a consultation, much less anything else, although she did see a couple of guys by the stage stripping the stairs.

She was contemplating the best way down there without ruining her Louboutin's or smudging her white dress when a rumbling engine pulled up outside. Maybe he thought being late would take her mind off the fact they were seriously behind on the restoration. It hadn't. He was about to find out why she was her mother's daughter.

She stomped out the front door and was halted by the blinding reflection bouncing off the windshield of a ginormous truck. It idled noisily as puffs of black carbon monoxide escaped the tailpipe.

Whoever was inside shut the environmental disaster down, letting it die with a harsh choke and cough. There was a weird static charge in the air around her, the driver's door swung open, and a tall hunk of handsome stepped out with a smile that had probably scared the father of every girl within a thousand miles of here.

Jared Martin.

She'd know that swagger anywhere. With a squeal of delight she flew down the stairs and launched herself into his tattooed arms, suddenly seventeen again instead of a twenty-seven year old interning cardiac surgeon.

"Well, would you look at who's all grown up?" Jared grinned as he swung her around before giving her a smacking kiss on the mouth. "About time you brought that pretty little backside of yours home."

"You're one to talk, Mr. World Traveler. Kyle tells me about you all the time. I heard your team had a super-hero complex," she teased, happy to see a friendly face.

"How is that butt-ugly brother of yours anyway? Last time I saw him he was fending off a group of Asian girls. And loving every minute of it."

"He's good. I think. We don't have news of him very often, and see him even less. He's supposed to get time off for the wedding, but I'll believe it when I see it."

Giving him a playful shove—which moved him not one inch—she glanced at the theatre doors. "Guess you heard the news then? I'm getting hitched in a couple of months. Can you believe it?"

Jared lifted her hand and inspected the solitaire nestled on her finger. "Well, the guy's got taste, and I'm not talking about the ring."

Katy pulled her hand away and tucked it behind her back. She'd argued with Jeff over the size of the stone, not that it did her any good. Turning away she changed the subject. "I've wanted to fix this old girl up for a long time." Her gaze ran over his familiar, yet different, face. "How about you, Jared? What's brought you back?"

The smile remained on his lips but disappeared from his eyes, and it was though a dark cloud passed before the sun. "It's hotter than Hades in Vegas this time of year. I decided to come home and make some peace with my past." He rubbed a work-roughened hand down her arm. "Maybe it's time you do the same?"

And that's when she knew. The hairs on the back of her neck and arms lifted. With an intuition she didn't know she had, Katy looked past Jared at his monster truck. Sure enough, the passenger door was open and a man had slid out while she'd been greeting her friend.

He'd always been larger than life, with his sky blue eyes glinting under a ragged ball cap, and hair the color of the finest champagne. She could see the stubble covering the lower half of his face and remembered how soft and yet bristly it felt against her breast.

Angry with herself for letting him get to her, she turned back to Jared with a grimace, "You could have warned me."

He shrugged uncomfortably, and shoved his hands into his pockets. "I gotta get to work. I heard the boss is a real hardass."

Jared flashed a warning look at the grimly silent man still standing near the truck. He hesitated, then gave her arm an awkward pat before striding into the building.

Leaving her alone.

With Ty Garrett.

CHAPTER TWO

On the steps of the theatre stood an angel gilded in white and gold. Her hair glittered like spun silk in the morning sun, while the filmy white dress she wore made him think of all kinds of sin. For once in his life, Ty Garrett was struck silent. He knew seeing Katy again would be hard, he just hadn't realized how cruel fate could be.

"Ty. I should have guessed."

He hadn't expected her to jump into his arms— though she'd seemed quite happy to do just that with Jared—but would it kill her to at least pretend she was glad to see him?

"You're late."

Apparently it would.

"Well you know me, sugar. Laggard that I am, getting up before noon is something of a stretch." If she wanted to think the worst, he didn't mind playing along.

"It's been a long time, Ty. You look... older." She brushed an impenetrable glance over him, rubbing at already raw emotions.

"You don't. You look like the same spoiled teenage brat you were the last time you stood on those stairs."

No way in hell was he going to admit seeing her again affected him. He'd learned his lesson. Give her an inch, and she'd take a mile.

Katy smiled—a Cheshire cat kind of smile—as though she knew anyway. "Well, now that we've gotten the pleasantries over with, do you suppose we could get to work? I have appointments to keep, even if you don't."

Yep, that was his Katy all right. Straight for the jugular. Except she wasn't his anymore, was she? He'd better remember that fact. Like he could possibly forget.

Tidal Falls' golden girl, voted most likely to succeed in the high school yearbook. And she hadn't proved them wrong. He'd received updates throughout the years on her academic prowess, and her subsequent appointment to one of California's premier cardiac hospitals. He was proud of her. Had never doubted her. Wish he could say she felt the same about him, but he knew better.

"Well, we'd best be moving inside then. I wouldn't want to mess up your precious schedule or anything," he growled, breathing in her peaches and cream scent as he shifted past her to hold the door open. Not that he needed a reminder; it already lived on in his memories.

Ty knew he was being an ass but couldn't seem to do anything to stop it. He'd only taken the job because he thought he'd be working with her old man to get the theatre ready for the precious wedding. His restoration business was just getting off the ground and a job like this wasn't one he could afford to pass up. Then he'd gotten the phone call from Mr. Fowler that Katy would be coming to town to handle the details. He'd come close to terminating the contract. The only thing that stopped him was the fact she'd know. She'd know she still affected him, controlled his actions. No way in hell's green acres was he admitting that to her. So here he was, hangover and all.

Katy opened her mouth to say something, then, shaking her head, strode past him into the cool interior of the old building. He needed to get his game face on. Pronto. He trailed behind, trying not to notice how her dress outlined her luscious bottom before tapering down to slender thighs. Her legs were as perfectly shaped as he remembered. His gaze dropped to feet encased in four-inch-kill-him-now shiny black heels with blood red soles, surely meant to stop a guy's heart.

And they worked.

He needed more coffee.

"I don't see how you're going to get this done in time. The place is a disaster zone. Do you want to explain why you're so far behind schedule?" She kept her back turned, her strawberry blond hair brushing her shoulders as she gazed around.

Ty also looked at the concession booth and entry ticket area. Where she saw incomplete walls and half-built counters, he envisioned the finished room in all its refurbished glory. For anyone who didn't understand the restoration business, it probably did look as though they'd never get finished. But for him it was like a work of art, each part coming together to form a piece of perfection. He'd get it done in time. What she didn't understand was this project meant as much, or more, to him as it did to her.

The Twilight Theatre.

The place where he'd fallen in love for the first, and last, time. His attachment to the old building began while he was still a scrawny kid sneaking in through the propped open back door to catch the last half of whichever Disney movie was playing on the matinee. Then, when he got a little older, it became the place to hang out with his friends on a Saturday night. They'd always sat in the back row, a bunch of kids, chucking buttery popcorn at the giggling girls a few seats down. In junior high he'd taken his dates there with plans to hit first base. The wide velvet-lined seats were perfect for groping hands in the dark. Amusement lifted one corner of his mouth. He remembered the many times he'd been caught in somewhat compromising positions by Mr. Fowler and his trusty flashlight.

It was on one such night that he first laid eyes on Katy Fowler. Her father had just found him and Melissa Foster making out in the middle row while Lethal Weapon played out on the big screen. With the flashlight aimed straight at them on high beam, he'd started his lecture on sins of the flesh. A young girl appeared at his side. Huge eyes, the color of spring, glinted from the shadows, and a flash of humor lit their depths at the predicament he was in. The little witch.

"Dad," her melodious voice was ripe with laughter. "Kyle says there's a problem with the projector and he needs you right away."

Obviously torn between finishing his speech and helping his son, he'd wavered for a moment until a flicker in the running film made his decision. He turned off the light, but only after a finger wag at the two of them, and took off through the curtains blocking the screen room from the front end.

After the drama had ended, Ty let loose a chuckle and leaned over Melissa's bodacious bod, holding out his hand. "Thanks. That was a little awkward."

The urchin grinned back. And when her slim fingers touched his, a little explosion traveled up his arm, fizzing like pop rocks in his chest.

"No problem. My dad seems to think he needs to teach everyone about the birds and the bees. You should see him when he gets on Kyle's back about it." As if she just realized she was talking to virtual strangers about sex, her face flamed a candy apple red.

"I better go. It was nice meeting you." She pulled away from his grip, turned, and sprinted up the aisle out of sight.

Ty had closed his fingers, capturing the residual warmth in his palm, and leaned back in his seat, oddly shaken by the whole encounter. He knew Kyle from school. Though a couple of years younger than Ty, they were on the same football team. He'd once mentioned he had a twin sister who drove him crazy. Ty could relate, he had two sisters and a brother of his own, all older and bossier. None that looked like Katy Fowler though.

"Wow, she's something, isn't she?" Came the amused, disdainful voice of his then girlfriend, Melissa.

"Yeah," he agreed. "She really is."

Ty was jerked back to the present by the sound of something crashing to the ground in the main gallery. Katy shared a startled look with him, and then they both raced for the curtained off area. Sweeping the tarpaulin aside, they were pelted by a big cloud of dust and debris. Choking on the haze, Ty motioned for Katy to stay put then worked his way down the aisle, cursing because he wasn't able to see a thing.

"Jared. Are you guys okay?" He reached the area where a five tier Venetian chandelier had crashed to the floor, sending shards of glass in every direction. Now that the dust was settling he could see Jared holding his arm, blood seeping between his fingers. After verifying no one else was seriously injured, Ty checked the damage.

"What the hell happened?" He started in his friend's direction, only to be shoved aside as Katy pushed by, disregarding both his stay back edict, and the precarious walkway.

"Let me see," she said, and peeled Jared's fingers back. He winced and she patted his shoulder. "Come on, tough guy. You can handle a little blood, can't you?"

"Depends on what you call little, Nurse Nightingale," Jared teased. "Where's your bedside manner?"

Ty wanted to make him bleed harder.

Disgusted, he turned away from the little tableau and stomped over to his other men. "You two all right?" At their nods, he frowned and gazed up at the hole in his ceiling. "What the hell happened? That light's been hanging there fine for fifty some-odd years, and suddenly it falls today?"

"I don't know, boss. We were working on the stairs going up to the stage and heard this big crack. Next thing you know the whole thing let go, and we dove for cover." Larry slapped his gloves against his thigh, dislodging a puff of dust from when he'd lunged out of the way. "We checked it just last week like you asked us. It was fine then—at least it seemed solid." He glanced over at Brent. "There's been some weird shit going on around here, lately."

Ty raked frustrated fingers through his hair. "What kind of *weird shit*? And why haven't you mentioned it before now?" He sighed, "I can't very well fix it if I don't know about it."

"Sorry, boss. We just figured it was kids playing pranks, is all." Brent dabbed at a cut across the bridge of his nose. "It started out pretty harmless. We'd go for a break and our lunches would be gone, or we'd head for the can and get locked in. That kind of stuff. Then a couple of days ago, Larry left to grab some parts and you stepped out to check on another job. I started on that molding you wanted lifted and was making good headway when the lights suddenly went out. It's some kind of fricken... beggin' your pardon." He nodded at Katy who'd come up beside Ty with Jared in tow. "Dark in here when those lights go out."

"It wasn't just a breaker?" Ty frowned, conscious of Katy's interest.

"First thing I checked. We wired all the sidelights into one panel box like you said, and put this chandelier in the other. They were both tripped. Now how do you suppose that happened?"

"Could it have been the same kids?" Katy asked.

"No ma'am, I don't see how. We have those panels in a locked room."

"We'll start keeping the entry doors secured at all times, see if that'll help," Ty said. "For now I'd better get Jared to the hospital. He's looking a little peaked." Then wished he'd kept quiet as everyone's attention, including Katy's, turned to Jared who looked anything but weak. More like badass, with his shirt wrapped around his forearm, and his sleeve of tats.

Jared raised his brow in a "seriously bro?" kind of way. In retaliation he looked at Katy and kind of wobbled. She, of course, raced over and tucked herself under his arm to hold him up, one hand resting on his flat stomach.

Then she sent Ty a disgusted glance, "Well if you noticed that he was weak, why didn't you come and help him? He's your friend."

She shepherded her patient up the aisle. "Let's go, Jared. My car is right outside, I'll take you to the hospital. You're going to need a few stitches for that cut."

About halfway up, Jared glanced back—and winked.

The prick.

CHAPTER THREE

Katy rolled down the windows of the car and let in the fresh autumn air filled with the scent of ripe apples and late blooming roses. Contrary to what they had hinted, the cut on Jared's arm wasn't serious, just a bit too deep to go without stitches. But she'd been happy to have the excuse to leave. To regroup.

"How are you holding up?" She kept one eye on the road while searching her favorite handbag—Prada—for sunglasses.

"Fine, until you did that," Jared grumbled. "Has no one ever taught you about the dangers of distracted driving?"

Her right hand found the hard-shell case and levered it out of her bag, while her left hand guided the car around a corner.

"I can also pat my head and rub my belly at the same time." She slid the frames up her nose and cast him a saucy sideways smile. "I'm multi-talented that way."

Her gaze skated over his well-defined abs bared by the T-shirt wrapped around his arm. "I see you've been working out since I saw you last."

"Gotta stay in shape to keep the ladies happy," he murmured, his focus on the houses zipping past. "You know the speed limit is thirty, right?"

Katy laughed, stress-free for the first time since she'd arrived. "I thought that was only a guideline."

Jeff's choice was for them to get married in California, surrounded by their friends and his family. But ever since Katy was young, she'd pictured herself getting married in her family's theatre. Something about the old place called to her.

Styled after the famous Loew's Theatre in Bridgeport, Connecticut, the hall was festooned with elegant maroon velvet curtains and an embossed dome ceiling showcasing a crystal chandelier glittering overhead like a Victorian lady in a fancy ball gown.

Katy had it all planned. She'd made up a scrapbook over the years filled with pictures. Dresses in a rainbow of colors. Flower arrangements of every make and description. Oh, and the cakes. The cakes were amazing, everything from chocolate ganache to lemony delight. Katy had a serious sweet tooth, and vowed her wedding would have as many of the decadent treats as possible.

Then there was the ceremony. The ancient beat of the wedding march and the bridesmaids leading the way to the stage. The best man in his black tuxedo would be her handsome brother, Kyle. Then Katy would follow, her father at her side. She could see herself gliding down an aisle covered with scattered rose petals, bouquet in hand. Her groom would accept her hand, his blue eyes moist...

Wait—Jeff had brown eyes.

She snapped back to the present, her fingers tightening on the wheel. She was over Ty Garrett, had been for a long time now. It must be a reaction to seeing him again, that's all. She didn't harbor any dreams they would suddenly realize all the time they'd wasted, declare their love, and ride off into the sunset together like some dumb romance novel.

Uncomfortable with her thoughts, Katy glanced over and caught Jared eyeing her speculatively.

"What?"

"Nothing. Just wondering what you've been doing the last few years." His hand patted the dash of her BMW. "You know, besides becoming a surgeon and planning a ritzy wedding, that is."

Katy's hackles rose.

She had fought this same reverse snobbery her whole life. Why did people always assume rich parents meant equally well-off children? She and Kyle worked for everything they'd achieved. Their parents had firmly believed in the *"learn the hard way"* rule.

For the most part Katy agreed with the edict, except when her brother really needed the help—and they'd refused. He quit school after that and disappeared. It was a couple of years before she heard from him again. He'd joined the Army Airborne jump school and became a freaking paratrooper, of all things. So yeah, it tended to tick her off when people thought they had it easy.

"You mean other than four years of undergraduate study, then four more years of med school, and now a five year residency to get my surgeon's ticket?" Sarcasm laced her voice. "I've been hobnobbing with California's rich and famous, of course."

Jared stretched across the console with his uninjured arm and awkwardly patted her shoulder. "Hey, whoa down tiger. I didn't mean anything by that. I'm proud of you. You're working toward accomplishing your dreams." His hand dropped into his lap and he turned to gaze out his side window. "That's more than a lot of us can say."

Katy drove a couple of blocks in silence. The neighborhoods they passed seemed the same as when she'd lived here, yet different somehow. The old hospital had been handy for everyone, situated in the center of town. Jared told her the new building was located on the west end, almost at the outskirts. As it came into view, Katy had to admit it was an impressive sight, easily twice as large as the old one. Modern in design, all rugged angles and glass with the roof covered in solar panels in an effort to save on energy consumption. A carport off to the side housed two ambulances and an emergency response truck.

She pulled into the visitor parking, found a space, and shut down the car's engine. Turning sideways, Katy waved her hand between them. "Okay, Martin. Spill the beans. What's going on with you?"

He fiddled with the makeshift bandage on his arm for a few moments before meeting her narrowed stare. "Nothing, it's just taking a bit to get my bearings after leaving the teams. You know how it is."

Yeah, she did. Her brother, still enlisted, showed many of the same symptoms. PTSD, Post-Traumatic Stress Disorder, a soldier's worst enemy. How do you fight against something that's invisible? Katy wished she had an answer. Thanks to Kyle she'd read up on the symptoms, one of which was the patient often felt alone, even surrounded by loved ones.

She reached over and punched his good arm.

"Ouch." His head reared back, and his eyebrows climbed for the ceiling. "What did you do that for?"

Katy smirked, "Just because. It's been a long time and I missed you, you big dork."

Jared's shoulders relaxed and his lips tipped upwards in a wry smile. "I can see why Ty was so hooked on you. You're kinda cute when you want to be."

Her pulse betrayed her, jumping at Ty's name. What was the matter with her? She wasn't some impressionable teenager to swoon at the mere mention of an old heartthrob. Those days were long past. And besides, she had a fiancé now and had no interest in talking about her non-relationship with Ty Garrett.

She shifted the conversation back to Jared. "When did you start working for Ty? Manual labor doesn't seem like your kind of thing. From what I remember, I expected to hear of you making it big in Silicon Valley with some great new invention."

Jared shrugged. "Your inner snob is showing. There's nothing wrong with making a living with your hands. Michelangelo did a damn fine job of it. Give Ty a break."

Katy snorted, she couldn't help it. "Are you comparing Ty's work with probably one of the most famous artists ever born?"

"Hey, don't knock it until you see it. He's pouring everything he's got into this project. I think you and your family are going to be pleasantly surprised when it's finished." He reached across and lightly flipped her hair.

Katy clicked her tongue. "You mean *if* it gets finished. There's not much time left before the wedding. Jeff will be here in another couple of weeks, and he's going to want to see some results." She straightened in her seat, pulled her keys, and stuffed them in her purse, then opened the door and climbed out.

Jared followed suit, and stared at her over the glistening black roof of the car. His eyes glinted with curiosity behind the lenses of his glasses. "When are you going to tell us something about this character, anyway?" His injured arm rested on the doorjamb. "Gotta admit I never pictured you with anyone but Ty. You guys always seemed perfect for each other."

She'd thought so too. Guess they were both wrong.

Katy shoved her door closed, and winced when it slammed shut. At Jared's raised brow, she lifted her chin in reply. "It's because your door is still open. And I have no issues with Ty. None at all."

He smirked, and closed his door—gently—before joining her on the sidewalk. He gave her a little shoulder bump and almost knocked her over.

"What? I don't have a problem, Ty is a friend, that's all. Now do you want to hear about Jeff, or don't you?"

She sidestepped a couple of giggling interns ogling Jared's admittedly fine physique. He barely noticed, his attention on her. That wasn't the Jared she remembered. He'd always been the ladies' man. Katy and her friend, Annie Campbell, were the only consistent women in his life besides his family.

"I've heard a little from Mom and Jack. They say he's a big-time property developer. That must make your pops happy," he said.

Yes, it had. Sometimes Katy wasn't sure if Jeff was dating her or her dad. "Aren't you a little chilly like that? I'm sure Ty could've lent you a jacket."

"Hey now, you hustled me out of the theatre before I had a chance to say boo. It's not my fault women find me irresistible," he smirked.

"In your dreams, buddy boy. In your dreams." They ambled toward the entrance. The cool breeze sent a chill up Katy's spine. "Jeff has a good business mind. His company seems to do very well for itself. He's a decent man, I'm sure you'll like him."

She glanced sideways and met Jared's dubious stare. "He cares about me." *Unlike Ty*, hung in the air between them.

"Katy..." Jared grasped her arm to slow her down.

Just then Doctor Johnson stepped out the front entry doors. Katy laughed and raced into his welcoming arms. She held on for a few seconds, inhaling the familiar scents of Old Spice and spearmint. He'd delivered her and Kyle into the world and in some ways, was more of a father to them than their own had ever been. Doc had often told the two youngsters they could be whatever they wanted, if only they dared to dream. Katy accredited her current career to the family doctor. He'd taught her the true value of becoming a physician, and it wasn't about the almighty dollar, no matter what her parents thought.

She gave his grizzled cheek a smooch, then stepped back to have a better look. He seemed just the same as she remembered. With a tall spare frame, dark twinkling eyes and thick salt and pepper hair, his friendly smile warmed the heart and instilled confidence in his patients.

He squeezed her fingers, and took note of Jared's arm. "Well, Katelyn Jane, it's been a while, hasn't it?. I've missed you, my girl."

"Oh, Doc, I've missed you, too. I should've visited more often." Quick tears rose to the surface.

"Hey now, let's have none of that." He tugged her in for another hug. "I know you and that brother of yours have a lot on your plate. I'm here whenever you need me, always will be. And besides..." He let her go and motioned Jared over, "you call me every month to check up on me. So it's not like you disappeared off the face of the planet—like this one did."

Katy smirked when six foot tall Jared cringed like a chastised child. "Sorry, Doc."

"And so you should be, young man. Your mother worried herself sick while you were gone." Doc Johnson's tone was firm with disapproval, while at the same time his hands gently unwrapped Jared's arm for a look. "Hmm, you'll need a few stitches for sure. Let's get you cleaned up, shall we?"

Kyle had mentioned that a few years earlier something had happened between Jared and his mother. Katy had discredited the info as gossip, but now she had to wonder if there was more to the story. She would try to talk to him after they left the hospital. Maybe that was the basis for his discontent. He'd always been a good friend, she wanted to help if she could.

"C'mon, let's get you inside before I have to carry you. I know how you SEAL boys are when it's proven you're human after all," she teased. "I like your new hospital, Doc. What made the town decide to shell out for new digs?"

"Hmm?" Doc Johnson looked rather bemused. "It wasn't the town, my dear. It was your fiancé."

CHAPTER FOUR

Frustrated, Ty swept up the broken glass with a corn broom and dumped the glittering pieces into a cardboard box. The old chandelier had hung in this theatre ever since he could remember. More than one kid had stared into its shining beauty and imagined himself a hero of fabled lands. Maybe a dragon-slayer, a spy, or even a covert agent. Ty had been all those at one time or another. Now all that history lay shattered at his feet.

He sighed. This job was becoming more problematic by the moment. He should probably call his brother and give him a heads up, but as sheriff, Jack already had enough on his plate. Besides, the two of them weren't getting along all that well lately. Jack couldn't understand why Ty had agreed to restore the theatre, considering his past with Katy. Hell, he didn't understand it himself.

Setting the broom aside, he strode up the ramp to the back of the room, pushed aside the tarp and made his way to the steel door marked, *Electrical*. He twisted the knob. Locked, just as it should be. He pulled a heavy set of keys from his pocket and searched for the one that fit. It was hard to see with the dim bulb above his head throwing his shadow up the walls. He needed a replacement for here also. He fed the key into the lock and had just started to turn the knob when a thud sounded somewhere behind him.

Startled, he swung around and stared at the two doors across the hall. The washrooms. He pushed open the women's first, not sure where the noise had come from. The room was pitch-black and oppressive. His heart gave a warning thump.

Tensed for anything, Ty felt along the wall for the switch. The light clicked on and he carefully made his way into the narrow rectangular room. Three sinks and a large mirror reflected the closed stalls across the way. He hesitated and then chose door number two first. He stood off to the side and slammed it back on its hinges, ready for anyone who might jump out at him.

Nothing.

Exhaling, he moved to the next stall.

Nothing again.

Ready to leave and check the men's restroom, Ty pushed the last door on his way by and jumped half out of his skin when a small brown body raced out between his legs.

What the...?

He searched for the critter, hoping like hell it wasn't a rat, and found two bright little eyes glaring at him from under the counter, partially hidden by the garbage can. Ty wrapped his fingers around the top and bottom of the container, ready to dump it over whatever was cowering in the corner.

Ty lifted the can.

The animal hissed and made a bid to escape, jumping over his boot and onto the counter where it slid into one of the sinks. He was left staring down at a shivering kitten, and his lips tilted wryly at his own fears. The poor thing couldn't be more than six weeks old and obviously scared silly. Topaz eyes tracked his every move from a mottled tortoiseshell colored body.

He tried to lift her out of the sink and cursed when razor sharp nails and teeth bit into his hand.

"Ouch, you little monster."

He yanked his hand back and frowned at the twin red tracks seeping blood down his finger. "What did you do that for?" His voice lowered to a soft lulling croon as he tried once more to pick the pint-sized runt up, with success this time. "I just want to check you out, little one."

Tiny paws rested on his index finger as Ty rubbed under the velvety chin. The kitten watched him warily for a few moments, then as if all the excitement had worn it out, her eyelids slid closed and her head tipped forward to rest on Ty's hand.

"How did you manage to land in here?" he murmured as he brushed gentle fingers down her bony back. Scrawny little thing. Her whole body easily fit in one hand. Good thing he'd planned on stopping at the store today anyway; looks like milk just got added to the shopping list.

Ty tucked her up against his chest then left the bathroom. He remembered to snatch his keys off the floor. They must have fallen out of the lock when he rushed for the source of the noise. The kitten opened sleepy eyes and let out the saddest little cry he'd ever heard, then promptly fell back to sleep.

"Where's your momma, hmm?" Ty stopped at the front counter where Brent was taking measurements for the new snack bar. "Look who I found hiding in the back room." Feeling like a proud papa, he held the kitten out to be admired.

Brent shoved the carpenter's pencil behind his ear and came around for a closer look. "Aw, looks like you've made a conquest there, boss." He grinned and tapped the creamy paw. "That's one homely cat."

Ty pulled the kitten back to the safety of his chest. He frowned, already oddly protective of his charge.

"She's a lot cuter than your ugly mug, Hansen. I'm going out for a bit. Lock up behind me."

There was a click of heels smacking together as he headed for the door. *Smartass.* No doubt he was getting the two-finger salute too. He never got any respect.

Those idiots didn't have a clue. From his spot hidden in the ductwork, he listened to them coo over that stupid kitten like a couple of pussies. He'd been a bit worried when he dropped the fur-ball from the ceiling in the bathroom that the fall would kill it. He could just imagine the scream if the boss's girl had gone in there and found a dead cat on the floor. This job was turning into the most fun he'd had in a while.

He pulled the impression he'd made out of his pocket. Perfect. It took a little longer than he expected for that chandelier to fall, but everything worked out in the end.

Just as he expected someone had come along to double check the electrical room, and he was there waiting. He'd dropped that kitten and grinned as it shook itself off, then scrambled across the room in a blind panic. Then he'd crawled the couple of feet on the rubber matting he'd laid out as a sound muffler and watched Garrett go all ninja on the bathroom door. Hilarious. Wish he'd taped it for later.

Knowing he only had a few moments, he'd dropped from the low ceiling, seized the keys from the lock, made his impressions, and swung back into place with time to spare. Now the games could really begin.

It felt good entering the hospital. Katy liked the cleanliness of the interior as much as she'd admired the architecture outside the building. She'd been surprised when Doc told her Jeff was the driving force behind the new hospital. Katy didn't think he'd listened when she talked about her hometown. Maybe he meant it as a gift to her. Their relationship had been a bit rocky lately. They were both very busy people and sometimes it was hard to find time for each other. She hoped that would change after the wedding.

They followed Doc Johnson, their shoes squeaking on the waxed floors, through the foyer and down one of the long hallways to the day-patient wing. She smiled at the attention Jared's lean body was getting from staff and patients alike, not that he seemed to notice.

Doc led them into a cubicle and pointed at a narrow steel bed along one wall. "Hop up there, and I'll be right back with the sutures."

Jared gave the bed a look between lowered brows and opted for leaning his bulk against the wall instead, his arms crossed over his chest.

Doc shook his head and patted Katy's arm on his way out the door. "Always did have attitude, that one."

Katy had to agree. Jared's emotions always ran close to the surface. If he was mad, you knew it. Unlike Ty. Every time they'd ever argued it'd been like trying to pour cold molasses out of a can to get him to talk. No go. Maybe that's why those two had managed to maintain their friendship all these years. It worked for them. It just hadn't for her and Ty.

"What's the matter, big guy? You scared of a little ol' needle?" she teased, as she wandered around the tiny room, built for functionality instead of comfort. Katy could easily have done the stitching herself, she'd certainly had more than enough practice during her internship, but it was better at the hospital where there would be a record of his visit in case of infection. Always better to be safe when it came to Worker's Compensation.

She could feel Jared's gaze follow her meandering path and wondered what was on her friend's mind. Katy moved to the detested steel examining table and hoisted herself up, swinging her legs like a child. "Talk to me, Jared. What's going on?"

Instead of a direct answer he turned the question back on her. "I could ask you the same. Any girl I've ever known who thought herself *in love*, couldn't quit gushing about it, but you, you haven't said a word." He straightened from the wall and ambled across to stand in front of her. "Shouldn't you be just a tad more excited, considering you're about to get married?" Jared picked up the hand wearing Jeff's weighty diamond ring and twisted it around to her palm. "Are you sure this is what you want, Katy Jane?"

Before she'd taken this trip into her past, the answer would have been a resounding yes. Jeff was handsome, smart, and dynamic. Everything she thought she wanted in a man. He wasn't grumpy, annoying, or aggravating, like a certain restoration man she knew. But Katy also couldn't discount her heart. The moment she'd seen Ty standing in a shaft of sunlight beside Jared's truck, she'd known she was in trouble. All the old feelings, long ago buried if not quite forgotten, had risen to the top like a shaken soda-pop. It took everything she had not to rush from Jared's arms into his. The only thing that stopped her was the dark frown on his too-handsome face the moment he caught sight of her.

"Of course I'm sure. I wouldn't be doing this otherwise." More than ready to change the subject, she glanced up through her lashes at Jared. "Other than Ty, have you run into any of the old gang yet? Like say, Annie Campbell?"

Jared froze for a split second, then let her hand fall back to her lap before swinging away. "Why do you ask about her?"

Hmm, that was interesting. Maybe the rumor mill was right this time. Katy had heard from her friend, Rebecca Sorenson, that Annie had been to see her and apparently when Jared's name came up in the conversation she'd blushed seven shades of red. The women planned to get together next week for Annie's birthday bash, so maybe she could pump her for info then.

"No reason, it's just nice to catch up, that's all. I hear Annie's been dating Ty's brother for a while now. Wonder if it's serious?"

That got the sparks flying. Jared spun around, glared at her, then turned for the door, all pent-up energy and no place to go. "What's taking so fricken long? I'm going to be healed up before they ever get around to sticking me."

Just then a nurse stepped into the room. She could have been a quarterback in another lifetime. Hands on broad hips, she stared them down with a bulldog expression. "I'm Nurse Spencer, which one's the patient?"

Katy smirked.

CHAPTER FIVE

Ty found an old blanket in the back of his truck, bundled it up and laid the kitten within the folds. It stared up at him with solemn gold eyes. "Don't look at me like that. I can't keep you. What am I going to do with a cat?"

Ty gave it a little rub behind the ear before starting his pick-up. "I'm hardly ever home. You'd be lonely." He glanced down as he shifted into gear and noticed the tiny claws kneading the blanket. "And besides, you'll ruin my furniture."

A couple of minutes later he signaled and pulled into the Pine Bluff Supermarket's parking lot. Being mid-day, the store wasn't packed with shoppers yet. He should be able to get in and out without taking too long. Other than the one little mew, the kitten hadn't made another sound but Ty still didn't want to leave it alone for long.

"I'll be right back. You protect the truck, okay, Tiger?" It stretched, gave a delicate little yawn and promptly went back to sleep. "Yeah, I thought not." He left the cat to its dreams and strolled across the lot, waving to Jared's mom as she turned from loading the trunk of her car.

"Hi, Grace, looks like you have quite a load there."

She wiped a slightly shaky hand across her brow and smiled up at him. "You know the restaurant business, we're always running short of one thing or the other." She slammed the lid down on the trunk and bundled her jacket around her rotund frame. "I heard you gave that boy of mine a job over at the theatre. How's he making out?"

Ty skipped over telling her of the accident, Jared could explain later. "It's great to have him back in town. I hope he sticks this time."

"Me too, son. Me too." She played with the strap of her purse for a couple of seconds, the breeze teasing a few wisps of graying hair about her flushed cheeks. "It's none of my business, and I probably should keep my trap shut, but with your history and all..." She sent him a mischievous look from her hazel eyes.

"Why don't you tell me what it is, and we'll go from there, okay?" Ty made a mental note to mention to Jared later that Grace wasn't looking her usual chipper self.

"Most likely it's nothing..."

C'mon Mrs. M.

Ty cut a glance over his shoulder at his truck, half-expecting to see Tiger glaring at him through the windshield. This morning's episode was just the latest in a string of bizarre occurrences. Yesterday his electrician, a guy who had worked with him for years, blew a gasket over some trivial shit and walked. Just like that. Good thing Jared had showed up for a job, because otherwise there wasn't a chance he'd get finished before the big day.

"There's a rumor floating around that Katy Fowler might be in town," she murmured. "Your Aunt Tess was talking to Pearl over at the Rendezvous Hotel and she mentioned that Katy had booked a room. I know you two have history and just thought you should be aware."

Wish he could say he was stunned, but that would be a lie. There are no secrets in a small town, only juicy gossip waiting to be discovered.

He decided to stop this particular rumor in its tracks. "Thanks, Grace. I appreciate your concern. And I've already seen her. She's here to oversee the plans for her wedding, and of course make sure the venue is ready on time."

He almost smiled at the disappointed look in her eyes. "I better get going. I found a kitten at work today. It's in my truck and I don't want to leave it for long." He took her cart to wheel it back to the store, and then remembered, "If you leave that stuff in your car, I'll stop around by the café on my way home and unload it for you."

A warm smile made her cheeks puff up like little red apples. She waved a hand to shoo him away. "Bless your heart, don't you worry about me. I have plenty of help. Are you going to keep the cat? I think Annie Campbell was looking for one to keep her old cat, Fitzroy, company."

Even though he'd been planning on giving the kitten up, Ty's immediate reaction was a resounding no. The little bag of bones already had a home, with him.

"Yeah, she's mine. She's kind of cute when she isn't clawing me half to death." He chuckled and carried on into the store.

Katy was tired and hungry by the time she dropped Jared home from the hospital. The stress of unexpectedly running into Ty had taken its toll. She'd anticipated seeing him at some point, but would have been happier if it had been on her terms. Instead, even though the theatre belonged to her family, she'd been the one left feeling like an interloper. Unwanted and out of place.

He'd changed. The ready smile and teasing remarks that used to charm her into his arms all those years ago, had been nowhere in sight today. He'd looked tired. Strained. There were dark shadows under his eyes and deep lines bracketed his lips.

Heat suffused her skin.

That mouth had mapped every inch of her body at one time. He'd been her first. The one no one else quite lived up to—not even Jeff, if she were honest with herself. Jeff was about as different from Ty as it was possible to be. Ty was light, with fair hair and complexion, Jeff was dark, half Native American, with black hair and swarthy skin. Where Ty was warm and caring, Jeff was often humorless and abrupt. But then his job was high-pressure like hers, so she understood. They were a lot alike; it's what attracted her in the first place. Jeff knew she was as tied to her cell phone as he was and that sometimes their personal life would have to take a backseat. It worked for them.

She wasn't anxious to go back to an empty hotel room, and decided to stop at the grocery store on the corner. It felt weird being back in her hometown and having to stay in a hotel, but her parents had sold their home when they moved to California.

A couple minutes later she pulled up near the doors and hopped out of the car, pausing to straighten her dress and smooth her hair. The old Mom and Pops store looked just the same as when her and Kyle had gone there as kids, anxious to spend their weekly allowances on the candy bins. She wondered if the same people owned it. She remembered them as kindly, with never a harsh word for the young customers invading their premises.

She entered with a smile on her lips, her thoughts full of happier times. But one glance down the aisle straight ahead changed that. Ty. What was he doing here?

She hesitated, not sure whether to duck back out or just hide in another part of the store until he left. Then another customer entered, brushing past her, and Ty looked up. She froze, caught in the icy cool depths of his eyes. Her pulse skittered around like a deer caught in a trap. Determined not to let him see her sweat, she hiked up her purse strap and sauntered toward him.

"Ty, I didn't expect to see you here. That's twice today. I'd almost think you had it planned." Her steps faltered when she realized just where he was standing— in front of the condom section. She flapped a hand in front of her face, a futile attempt to calm her racing pulse and pink cheeks.

He eyed her embarrassment for an amused moment before leaning over and deliberately picking up a box of extra large—in his dreams—glow in the dark— really?—contraceptives. "Funny, that's what I was going to say." He dropped the box into the half-full basket he carried in one hand. "After all, sugar, I was here first."

Her gaze helplessly followed the carton of Trojans. They landed on top of three cans of kitten food, various colorful toys, and some litter. Katy reached into the basket and plucked out a toy mouse. "Unless you're into some kinky activities, Garrett, your cover is blown." She pointed toward the shelves behind him filled with pet supplies.

He shrugged. "You're the one who leapt to conclusions."

She didn't think he was talking about the condoms. There was no sense in bringing up the past; it could only dredge up the hurt all over again. Besides, she'd moved on, they both had if the size of that box was anything to go by. Desperate to get the picture forming in her head to disappear, Katy searched for a safe topic.

"So, whose cat are you buying for?" Then a horrifying thought entered her mind. What if he had a girlfriend? Or even a wife? She hadn't heard of him getting married, but that didn't mean it hadn't happened. "Never mind, it's none of my business. That basket looks heavy. I'll let you get back to your…" she couldn't help it, her eyes slid to the contraceptives, "shopping. I need to get going anyway."

Katy whirled on her spiked heel, and was halfway down the aisle when Ty's voice stopped her. "The kitten is mine, Katy. If you want to have a look, it's in my truck right now."

She turned, her heart lightened by his words. It was wrong, this desire to spend time with an old school flame. But after all, you couldn't get much more innocent than a kitten, right?

Brushing aside Jeff's stern countenance, Katy smiled, "I'd love to."

CHAPTER SIX

This was so far past being a good idea, it wasn't even in the ball park. Ty trailed Katy out of the grocery store, the kitty litter under one arm, while the condoms burned a hole in the bag he held in his other hand.

What the hell was he thinking?

The breeze teased the ends of her hair and carried the scent of autumn's harvest to his starved senses. Peaches, pears, and apples—*yum.* Her white dress played homage to a truly world class heart-shaped ass. And the blood red soles of those shoes of hers were going to drive him around the bend. He could picture her on his bed, pink skinned and inviting, wearing nothing but those heels.

He coughed to clear a suddenly parched throat. She glanced around and he had to quickly move the bag so it would cover the bulge in his jeans. Ty pointed the way to his truck with his chin, anxious now to get this over with and escape from his self-imposed torture.

"It's the white Dodge over in the corner."

Katy nodded. "Good, you parked in the shade. It's surprising how many people don't think to do that when they have their pets in the vehicle."

Then she got a glimpse of Tiger yowling from its spot on his dash. "Oh, Ty, she's so tiny." Those four-inch heels clicked into overdrive as she hurried to his truck and tried the locked door handle. "Open up, she's scared, the poor thing." Her hand flattened against the glass as if sheer willpower alone could let her inside.

Ty juggled his packages so he could drag the remote from his pocket. A double-click later all four doors were unlocked and Katy was leaning over his seat to reach the kitten. The back of her dress crawled into the danger zone, showing off her long, long legs.

Sweet hell.

His brow broke out in a prickly sweat.

"C'mon, honey, I won't hurt you. You're so pretty, yes you are. Come here, sweetheart."

Ty muffled a groan. Katy's crooning just about did him in right there. He wasn't sure how Tiger held out, because if she used those words on him in that husky, sexy tone... he wrenched open the back door and dumped the groceries on the floor. A long, deep sigh later he closed the door, placed his hands on Katy's waist and gently moved her aside.

"Here, I'll get her." He climbed into the four-by-four and scooped the recalcitrant kitten into his hand. "Hey there, Tiger, good job protecting the truck. Come say hi to the pretty lady, and no scratching."

He nuzzled his nose into its soft, furry neck and then passed her down to Katy's waiting hands, their fingers tangling for a too brief moment.

"Hello, beautiful. What are you doing with this guy, huh?" She burrowed her face right into the same spot he had and everything inside him tightened painfully. She was killing him here.

"You find that hard to believe, right?" he grumbled.

She glanced up, her mossy green eyes soft with affection. "What?"

His fingers wrapped around the steering wheel before he did what he craved. Bury his hands in that silken waterfall of hair, drag her close, and see if her neck was half as soft as the cat's. "That anyone would want to stay with me of their own volition?"

Katy frowned. "What are you talking about? I was teasing, Ty. Don't make this into something it's not."

Words to live by.

He enviously watched her slender fingers caress the kitten until it fell into a light doze. Lucky cat.

"Where did you get her?"

Ty's gaze rose to her lips. His inner sensor shut down, and the invitation erupted from his traitorous tongue before he had time to think it over. "Come for dinner and I'll tell you."

The words hung in the air, accompanied by little bubbles of mistrust, betrayal, and attraction. This was a mistake. Whatever happened between the two of them years ago, it had ended in a spectacular explosion he wasn't in any hurry to recreate.

He opened his mouth, about to tell her to forget it, but instead became hooked by the swirling confusion in her jade green eyes. Instead of brushing her off, which would've been the smart move, he ended up practically begging.

"Please."

He was so screwed.

Katy couldn't believe she was actually contemplating taking Ty up on his offer. What was that old adage? If you play with fire... oh, but the heat was an addiction. Her gaze danced over broad shoulders stretching the seams of his denim shirt across his back. And his muscular arm, highlighted by the folded sleeves, draped over the leather steering wheel with work-roughened fingers that were thick and calloused from hours of labor. So very different from Jeff's clean, manicured hands.

This was crazy.

She looked away, across the parking lot, to give herself a moment to breathe. The trees wore their fall dresses in fiery reds, pumpkin orange, and lemony yellow. A big grey squirrel ran down the trunk of a Maple. It paused for a cautious moment, and then grabbed a nut before scurrying up the tree, chattering a warning to birds and humans alike. A warning she should heed.

Katy turned back, a glib excuse to turn him down on the tip of her tongue, when kitten-little decided it was time to wake up. Her sharp nails dug into the soft skin of Katy's inner arm. "Ouch, Chester, let go."

"Chester? What kind of pansy name is that?" Ty smirked.

"Well, it's more original than Tiger." Katy giggled, and just like that she changed her mind. "Dinner sounds good. I'll follow you there so you don't have to go out later."

Refusing to overthink her decision, she untangled herself from the kitten's claws, gave it a peck on the head, and handed her over to Ty's outstretched hand.

"Come're you little monster," he grumbled, but handled the tiny body with the gentlest of touches. "You're going to be more trouble than your worth, I'm thinking."

He returned the animal to its nest of blankets, and then turned back to Katy. She had the distinct feeling he wasn't just talking about the cat. The complicated mix of reactions she could see reflected in his eyes like storm tossed clouds, contrarily made her feel somewhat better. At least she wasn't alone in this tempest of emotion filling the air between them.

He cleared his throat. "It's not a problem if you want to leave your car here. Your *boyfriend* might not approve of you visiting another man's home. If your car is sitting in my driveway, someone's sure to notice."

Katy's brows lowered at his tone. She admitted to being curious about his home and wasn't going to be put off that easily. Ten years was a long time. He'd been on her mind often over the years. It bothered her they had never actually said goodbye to their relationship.

"He's not my *boyfriend*, as you so inelegantly put it, he's my fiancé. And he wouldn't mind, because he trusts me." She stepped back, shut his door, and waited for him to lower the window. "Are you cooking me some dinner, or am I going to a take-out place?"

Ty stared at her for a moment, then leaned over and fired up the engine. "Follow me." But then he ruined it by murmuring, "Said the spider to the fly."

Katy hurried over to her car before he changed his mind and left her behind. She didn't want to delve too deeply into why it was suddenly so important to remain in his company for a while longer, but she couldn't deny that it was.

They toured through a few residential neighborhoods, even passing by her friend, Rebecca's house. Katy talked tough, but there was no reason to go and test her theory if it wasn't necessary. Jeff did trust her. She knew that. It was more a question of how much did she trust herself?

Ty's brake lights came on as he slowed for a paved drive along a tall stand of Cedars. At the end of the drive a low-slung rancher style home blended beautifully into the surrounding landscape. Finished with sandstone siding and lots of tall windows, the home looked warm, welcoming, and oh-so-familiar. Ty had bought their house. The one she'd dreamed of them owning one day. Did he remember?

Katy pulled up behind just as he stepped from the vehicle. Her headlights highlighted his long jean clad legs and lip-smacking tight butt. She gulped. *Oh, man.* He looked even better than when they were teens, more masculine, assertive—virile. She opened the door without conscious thought. His magnetism drew her to him as sure as the sun sets in the west. It probably always would.

He waited near the front of his pick-up, the kitten comfortably held in the crook of his arm. His face looked forbidding, as though now he'd had time to think about it he regretted inviting her. Too bad, she was here and she had no plans on leaving until they talked. The next few weeks would be stressful enough without having Ty glowering every time she stepped into the same room.

Her hand fanned out, encompassing the house and surrounding yard. "So this is it, your kingdom?"

His mouth quirked and a hint of that dimple she lo… liked so much, made an appearance. "You remember that, do you?"

She remembered everything.

"Of course. You never shut up about it. I think Jared and I must have heard at least fifty times about how much you wanted out from under your brother and sisters shadow. How, one day you were going to have your own little kingdom where you would call the shots." She smiled at the memory. "You always did hate being the youngest in your family."

Ty snorted. "Can you blame me? My sisters are beautiful, smart, and well-liked. And Jack… Jack has a Goddamn hero complex. First he became a football star, and now he's the sheriff of our hometown. How's a guy supposed to compete with that?" He turned away and strode toward his front door; obviously sorry he'd said anything.

Katy hurried to catch up. "It's not supposed to be a contest, Ty. Your family *is* pretty amazing." Then, when he glanced back at her with a thanks-for-nothing eye roll, she added, "But, so are you." She reached out and clasped his forearm. "Seriously, you are. You've never given yourself enough credit. What about all the endeavors you've accomplished, don't they count for anything?"

She squeezed his arm and drowned in the deepening blue of his gaze. Her heart gave a little kick, suddenly conscious of how close together they stood. The muscles under her palm flexed and her breathing quickened. She dropped her hand as if it were on fire and took a step back.

"Anyway, enough preaching. Show me your house."

"Katy."

Ty made a move toward her, stopping the air in her lungs, but then he shook his head and turned away to unlock the door. He flicked on the lights and moved aside to let her enter first. As she slid past, Katy glanced up and then away, her skin growing hot at the hunger glowing in his eyes.

She gave herself a stern talking to even as she took in the beauty of his home. Though it possessed a masculine stamp with the oversized furniture and dark colors, Ty had made himself a perfect sanctuary to come back to after a long day's work. The walls were a soft pastel blue, a good foil for the walnut flooring. A bay window at the far side of the room looked out over a private fenced yard, a bricked patio, and a Jacuzzi tub.

She could all too easily picture Ty stepping out of that steaming pool toward her. Katy's temperature rising as he strode toward her, water dripping off that powerful, sexy, *bare* body. She would offer to help dry him, inch by spectacular inch. Her hands tingled with the imaginary sensation of smooth skin and rippling muscles. Her tongue…

A cough from behind had Katy spinning from the glass, her face a bright red.

Ty looked at her quizzically for a moment before pointing to another door. "The bathroom's through there if you'd like to freshen up. I'm just going to take

Tiger here and get her settled in the porch." He rubbed the kitten's head. "I'll start dinner, and then we can have that talk."

Katy nodded and turned away, grateful for the reprieve. She closed the bathroom door and flipped the light switch. A flushed face and hectic eyes stared back at her from the beveled mirror. She bent and splashed cold water from the brass faucet over her heated cheeks.

This had to stop.

The diamond solitaire winked at her under the bright lights, reminding her of her obligations to another man. And why was she suddenly thinking of her marriage to Jeff as an obligation? Why did her father hire Ty and bring him back into her world? She'd done fine without him all these years. Really. Her hard won career was taking off. She had a beautiful condo near the beach. A gorgeous fiancé. Life was great.

So don't screw it up.

Great advice. Now if she'd only follow it. Katy finished drying her hands, pulled her brush out of her purse and dragged it through her hair. Touched up her lipstick with a slightly shaky hand, and opened the door like she was headed to the gallows. The light on the far side of the living room beckoned, guiding her toward the mouthwatering smells of garlic, onions, and Italian seasoning.

The sight of Ty standing guard over a bubbling pot of pasta while stirring a sauté pan of sauce at the largest stainless steel stove she'd ever seen, made Katy smile. This Ty she felt comfortable with. While dating they'd often spent their evenings together preparing gastronomic delights at home instead of going out to some swanky restaurant. She remembered how he said cooking relaxed him. This was a chef's domain, from the butcher-block counter with the brass-bottomed pots hanging above, to the giant French door refrigerator. She had kitchen envy.

"Wow. This is nice, Ty." She smiled when he glanced over his shoulder. "It must be hard to drag yourself away for work."

"Some days." He nodded toward the fridge; "There's plenty of salad fixings in the crisper, go crazy." His gaze did a slow sweep of her body. "I seem to remember you like your greens."

Which was a polite way of saying she'd always worried about her weight. They'd had numerous arguments on the subject. He'd maintained a proper diet was key to good health, while she'd argued everything a body needed could be found from the earth. She wasn't a vegan, but could understand the draw.

"And I remember you love a good steak, the redder, the better." She opened the crisper and withdrew romaine, spinach, radishes, carrots, a pint of strawberries, and some balsamic vinegar. For a while there was a peaceful silence as they worked together to make dinner. Katy was just in the process of cutting up the berries when Ty joined her at the counter.

"Anything I can do?" He picked up a sliced strawberry and popped it into his mouth.

"Hey, leave my fruit alone," she warned, teasing. He reached for another and she grasped his wrist, laughing. It petered out at the naked craving in his gaze.

He brought the strawberry to her mouth, and when she didn't open quick enough, he did a slow glide across her lips. Her tongue flicked out to catch a drip and he groaned, the low sound stroking across every nerve in her body.

"You're killing me," he muttered, and his mouth hovered ever closer, teasing. Just before they made contact she thought she heard, "but what a way to go."

CHAPTER SEVEN

Ty would always remember his first taste of heaven. A warm honeyed mouth coated in sweet juicy berry. Soft pillowy breasts and the silken slide of peach scented hair. The breath-stealing feel of her hourglass figure beneath his hands, and the sexy little cries she couldn't quite control. A gauge that told him better than any words how much she wanted him.

His heart thundered like an Indy car on a perfect oval track. If he didn't slow this down soon, Ty worried he'd crash and burn. Been there, done that. Had the scars to prove it, thank you very much.

His lips refused to listen though, bad lips. They were intent on mapping every crease and crevice of her mouth, inside and out. Powerless against the onslaught of memories mixing with the uncertain present, Ty gave up on backing away. Instead he delved within, on a mission to replace another man's kisses. Determined to stamp his mark upon her soul.

He couldn't seem to fill up on her taste; it reminded him of a decadent dessert. He knew it was bad for him, but lacked the strength to set it aside. One more lick here and a nibble just there, at the cupid's bow of her lip. When her tongue flicked out to soothe the ache, Ty sucked it into his mouth in a game of tag where they both came out the winner.

His hands performed braille on every inch of skin they could reach. From curvy hips to the underside of her more-than-a-handful breasts, there wasn't a spot he didn't crave to relearn. He loved the little breathy catch, then sigh, she did every time he came to a particularly sensitive area. Like now, when his fingers spread out over her ribcage while his thumbs lightly tweaked hardened nipples.

His lips worked a path along her jawline to the shell of her ear, and he smiled when her head fell back to grant him more access. He well remembered her sensitivity to this erogenous zone on her body. Her skin was velvety soft, nearly translucent. He could almost feel the blood pulsating through her veins beneath his lips. His own heart throbbed in response, speeding along his cells to pound a message to his engorged cock. *Take her, take her now.*

His arm swept out and shoved the salad bowl aside. Ignoring her startled gasp, he lifted her onto the counter and edged between her legs.

"Ty," she hesitated, her hands on his shoulders to hold him at bay. "We shouldn't."

Caught in a cloud of lust, it took him a bit to comprehend her words, and a much longer moment to admit the validity. His head dropped and he heaved a frustrated sigh.

Her hand came up and brushed gentle fingers through his hair, and he leaned into her touch, helpless to resist.

"Ty, I'm sorry. I didn't mean to lead you on." He raised his head and met her worried gaze. A ghost of a smile touched her lips. "On the kitchen counter? Really?"

He laughed, then groaned at her bemused expression. Time to step back before he showed her just how possible it could be. He leaned forward and gave her one last, lingering kiss, then turned back to his now overdone noodles. Yep, there had to be a metaphor in there somewhere, for sure.

"If you set the table, I'll finish up in here." He glanced over his shoulder to make sure she made it off the counter safely, just in time to see her dress ride up her thighs as she levered herself down. And there it was, that tempting little swan-shaped birthmark of hers. He'd teased her about it often enough. That it was their private spot, a secret only they—and her parents—knew about. Guess that wasn't true anymore.

Angry with himself for still giving a shit, Ty grabbed for the pot of pasta, remembering too late that he needed potholders. The heat from the steel handles sizzled against his palms. "Ouch, shit," he swore, and let go. The liquid sloshed, hissing as it hit the hot burner.

"What happened? Are you okay?" Katy's worried tones as she rushed to his side only embarrassed him. What a lame-brained thing to do. If a bare leg was all it took to ruin his concentration he was in trouble. Ty refused to admit it was anything more than that; he couldn't afford to get sucked into Katy's orbit again. He still hadn't recovered from the last time.

"I'm fine." He grimaced as she turned his hands over and examined the deep red slashes embedded in his palms.

"Oh, Ty, that looks painful." Her finger lightly traced the outer edge of the mark, leaving its own brand upon his skin. "I think you should run some cold water over them. Do you have any burn salve?"

She led him to the sink and turned on the tap before guiding his hands beneath the spray. His arms jerked with the shock of cold against overheated flesh.

Shit, that hurts.

"I think there's some in the bathroom cabinet, but I'll be fine." *After you leave.* Nothing a good shot of whiskey couldn't cure, except he was trying to quit. Oh well, tomorrow was another day.

"Don't be silly. I'll be right back. Keep your hands under there, okay?" She waited for his nod before letting go to slip from the room.

Now he was going to have to handle her playing Nurse Nightingale on him, was this night never going to end? Ty just wanted to lick his wounds, literally and figuratively, alone. He'd liked the thought of having her in his home, but now was almost sorry he'd invited her. How could he ever look at that counter again without picturing her laid out for him like the sweetest of delicacies? Or think of her silhouette against the picture window in his living room; an angel, come to life just for him.

The coolness of the water was working its magic and deadening his hands to the pain. Wish it were that easy to numb a bruised heart. He gazed at the twin trails of reddened skin, grateful that the burn seemed superficial. He was already on an impossibly tight schedule; the last thing he needed was to have his hands screwed up. The work on the stage was set to begin next week, and thanks to his electrician quitting on him, he was already short-handed. Good thing Jared had come back home and needed a job. He was the best Ty had ever seen with wiring and computer programming. With his friend on board, Ty had a good chance of his vision for the old theatre turning into a reality.

"All I could find is this aloe cream, but it should help." Katy said, coming up behind him and laying a warm hand on his shoulder. "How's it feeling?"

Ty controlled his flinch at her touch, shut off the water, and turned away to grab a hand towel. "It's fine now, the water did the trick. I think I'll wait until later to apply the ointment. You ready to eat, I'm starved." He avoided her uncertain stare and opened the cupboard for plates, setting them on the spot her sweet ass had covered moments ago. Shit, her dress. He hadn't even thought of it at the time, but she'd just been cutting greens up there. Not the best combination with white. "How's your dress?"

"What?" She looked perplexed for a second, and then the light bulb went off. It was kinda cute, actually. Her hands groped her butt—lucky hands—and her head swiveled this way and that, trying to check out the damage.

"Turn around, let me have a look." He chuckled.

She gave him the fish-eye stare, then slowly twirled on those stiletto heels of hers. "Do you have any idea how much this dress cost me, Ty Garrett?" Her hair whirled outward like a ray of sunshine as she swung her head to glare at him over her shoulder. "Well? Is it stained?"

Ty just shook his head, at a loss for words.

Sweet Jesus.

There, right at the apex of her thighs, lay the mark of Cain. A bright red strawberry clung to the snowy white cloth like a bull's-eye, defying gravity and angry woman. And like a sheep led to slaughter, he couldn't resist the lure.

Katy's eyes widened in shock when Ty fell to his knees behind her and grasped her hips so that she couldn't move. "Ty, what are you..." The rest of the words dried up and floated away at the touch of his mouth. An unbidden moan crawled up her throat and her knees went weak. The only things holding her up were those insidious hands. They slid down the front of her legs to the bottom of her dress and then under, working their way slowly, oh so slowly, up her inner thighs. His teeth were taking little erotic nibbles designed to make her lose her sanity.

"Ty," she breathed, his name a prayer on her lips.

"Shh, I've got you," he murmured, and every nerve quivered with longing.

Her head fell forward and she helplessly, hopefully, watched those fingers inch closer and closer to nirvana.

Then they were there. Touching, caressing, delving. His mouth nipped and sucked and it all became too much. She closed her eyes and let the sensations wash over her, the excitement, the soaring, the bliss.

When she came back to earth, it was to find herself lying beside Ty on the floor of his kitchen, his somber eyes cataloging her features.

"You're so fricking beautiful." His hand reached out and tucked a wayward strand of hair behind her ear.

Now that the glow was slowly fading, Katy was horrified. She'd just cheated on her fiancé. Well, not technically, but close enough to matter. Why did she agree to come to Ty's house?

"This is a mistake." The words exploded into the air between them, too late for her to take them back.

Ty's hand stilled before dropping to his side, a look of such contempt crossing his face that she shrunk away. He turned onto his back and folded his arms behind his head with a façade of indifference. Katy knew better, she'd hurt him. She hadn't meant to, but that didn't help the situation. All she could do was try to make him understand.

"Ty..."

"I think you better go. You don't want to have the neighbors talking anymore than they already are." He rolled to his feet, full of frustrated energy. "Come on, I'll walk you to the door."

"Ty, please, just listen," she pleaded, climbing up awkwardly, unaided.

"No," he snarled. Then, in a slightly quieter tone, "There's nothing left to say. Let's forget this ever happened. I'll finish my job, you'll get married, and we'll all live happy fricken after." He turned away and strode through the living room to open the front door. "I wish I could say it's been a pleasure, but only one of us achieved that particular plateau."

Katy stomped after him. The man seriously knew how to piss her off. "Okay, I'll go. When you're ready to act like a grown-up, we can talk this out. I want to explain but not when you're being so childish."

"Ha, that's a good one. You want childish? How about the girl who said she loved me, but instead when mommy and daddy said it's him or us, she ran like the little princess I always knew she was? That, *baby*... is childish."

Katy's mouth dropped open. All these years, and that's what he'd been thinking? *Oh, Ty.* She lifted her hand, palm up in entreaty, but he'd already closed the door in her face. And that's when she realized he'd somehow maneuvered her onto the porch.

CHAPTER EIGHT

Katy stirred to the sound of her cell phone trilling from the bedside table. Eyes still blurry, she rolled over and brought the phone to her ear. "Ty, I'm glad you called."

She'd fallen asleep with his name on her lips. Good, maybe he was sorry and wanted to talk now.

"Who's Ty? You fooling around on me, sweetheart?" Jeff's polished voice had her sitting up and clutching the blanket to her breast.

She rubbed tired fingers over her scalp, brushed the hair back from her face, and frowned at her pale reflection in the mirror across the room. "Jeff. You surprised me. I thought you were busy in meetings for the next few days."

"Not so busy I can't take a minute to call my fiancé and wish her a good morning."

His intimate tone jarred. She'd never noticed that before. After a restless night spent tossing and turning, the artificial dimness caused by the hotel's lined curtains allowed her to fall asleep sometime around dawn. Maybe that's all this was, crankiness due to a lack of sleep.

Yeah right.

Katy sighed. It was hardly Jeff's fault she couldn't get to sleep. No, that honor was reserved for a certain exasperating, too-proud-for-his-own-good man she knew.

"So, are you going to answer my question? Who is this Ty character, and why were you expecting his call?" Jeff asked, his impatience seeping down the line. She could hear office noise in the background; printers and fax machines, telephones ringing and employees arriving for another day of buy and conquer in the corporate world. Which reminded her...

"He's the contractor Dad hired to fix up the theatre, remember?" She wished he would try to understand how important this was to her. But to Jeff, it was nothing but a waste of time. He felt getting married in a fancy hotel with a gazillion people they didn't even know was the *right* image for an up and coming entrepreneur.

"Yeah, whatever you want, babe. Listen, I have to go. I'll call you later and you can tell me all about it." There was a hushed murmur of voices, and then he came back online, "Have fun, and I'll see you sometime next week." Click.

"Wait..."

Katy let the hand holding the cell drop to her lap. "Love you, too."

She wanted to know why he'd decided to build a hospital here, in her hometown, but hadn't thought to mention it. She appreciated the gesture, especially since Tidal Falls was long past due needing updated facilities. Maybe he'd meant it as a surprise.

The soft hum of the air conditioner and the occasional muted clang of a door closing down the hall were the only sounds in the room. She fell backward and let her head hit the pillow with a whoosh. Lavender scented the air from the sinfully soft Egyptian cotton sheets. Wonder what kind of sheets Ty used. Probably silk. And why that should make her squirm, she wasn't going to think about. Much.

Her gaze followed the lazy clockwise turn of the ceiling fan above her head. Inevitably her thoughts turned to the night before. With little effort she could once again see the hot light flare in Ty's eyes just before he lowered his lips to hers and turned her world upside down. Her skin heated as she recalled her response to his kisses. Her pulse tumbled in reaction to the exquisite touch of his hands upon her breasts, his complete mastery of her body.

And to the hurtful words like poisoned darts they'd exchanged in the end.

Katy rolled over and hugged the spare pillow, wishing for a pair of strong arms and a sturdy chest to hold her. And it wasn't her fiancé she missed. Maybe this was a case of pre-wedding jitters, nothing to get her knickers in a knot over. Perfectly normal, in fact. What she needed was to get up, have a shower, and like Ty said, forget this ever happened.

She could give Rebecca a call and see if they could get together for lunch. She hoped her friend would agree to be a bridesmaid on short notice. Katy had wanted to ask her sooner, but Jeff insisted his sisters needed to be in the bridal party so… then his youngest sister, Nikki, ran away with her boyfriend to backpack across Europe. Jeff had gone ballistic, but Katy was secretly happy for the young woman. Their parents had died in a plane crash a few years earlier, leaving Jeff to care for a fledgling corporation and three young girls. A tall order for any man, but he'd buckled down and succeeded better than anyone could have foreseen.

Katy met him when her mother had commissioned his company to add a wing to the hospital. Tall, dark, and handsome, he'd stood out amid all the white-coated doctors in his expensive three-piece suit and tie. She'd been drawn to his quiet self-confidence and charm. They'd dated for a couple of years before he popped the question and she'd said yes, sure that she'd met her perfect match.

She was still sure. Ty was an anomaly. Something she could, and would, control.

Ty spent the morning at the local welding shop. He had a firm dream in mind of a stage that could lift and lower three levels by the power of hydraulics. With the ability to rise to stage level, lower to audience level, or disappear as an orchestra pit the theatre would be multi-purpose, allowing for live, as well as on-screen performances.

When he'd first come up with the plan everyone called him crazy. What did Tidal Falls need with a live theatre? The school gymnasium had done the job for years, hadn't it? And they were probably right. He was an idiot for taking this on. But once he had it in his head, he couldn't seem to let it go. Mr. Fowler had given him carte blanche as long as he had it finished in time for his daughter's wedding and Ty took responsibility for the costs until the project was finished. He had a lot resting on this venture, but if it came out the way he envisioned... Katy would be stunned.

He shook his head, this obsession with her needed to end. She wasn't his anymore, hadn't been in years. Maybe if he hadn't fallen so hard. But right from the first moment he met her in the dusky intimacy of the theatre, with her laughing green eyes and mischievous smile, he'd been hooked. It had taken a long time to recover after she left, and even longer before he considered dating again. No one else could hold a candle to her.

And now she was back.

"Okay, that's got 'er." Mitch's voice was overloud now that the frying bacon noise of the welding had stopped. The air was thick with smoke and the aroma of hot metals freshly fused together.

"What took you so long?" Ty turned his head from his position of holding the piece in place and admired the precision of the weld. "Just kidding, good job." He pulled off a glove and grimaced at the pain. The burn had faded from a flaming red to a pale pink but still remained tender.

His friend lifted the helmet off his matted hair and grinned at him, a black streak on his cheek highlighting his pearly whites. "What did you expect? When you have the best…"

"Yeah, yeah, I know," Ty answered, "forget the rest." If only he could reverse that a little in his personal life. His motto should be, forget the best, so you can accept the rest.

"Have you seen her yet? I heard she was back in town." Mitch turned away to set the stinger down.

There was no question who he meant. The whole town knew of Ty and Katy's past. They were probably ears to the wall waiting for the implosion. Too bad he'd have to disappoint them.

"She came and looked the job over yesterday. She's worried we won't get done in time, which is why I'm here busting your scrawny ass today." Ty's lips curled at the misnomer. Mitch was six-five, two hundred-eighty pounds, and built like a brick shithouse. He'd played football with Jack and even got a scholarship to college out of it, but then the accident with Jack happened and those dreams came to a screeching halt.

"Well, unless you add another tier or something we should be able to squeak in under the wire." Mitch said. "And get that glint out of your eye, the answer is no." He raised a dismissing hand, strode to the counter, and poured a cup of three-hour-old coffee. "You want to go for a beer?"

Ty wanted to agree, except it was barely noon. "Why don't you let me buy you lunch instead? I'm starving." Especially since he'd thrown out last night's dinner after Katy left.

"Yeah, sure, man. Just give me a few to wash this sweat off and we can go." Mitch set the blackened cup down and left the room.

Ty wandered around the brightly lit shop checking on their progress. It was coming together, the picture in his head now taking form. This was the part of the restoration business he loved. Incorporating new and old into seamless functionality. The old theatre would be the flagship for his line of work. He'd done many residential jobs, but this would be his first commercial project. It could open doors for his business and allow for expansion. So far he'd worked from home but Ty wanted to open a store where he could carry his own line of merchandise. Homemade furniture, expertly crafted and made to last. Kitchen cupboards manufactured by hand with love and care. Commissioned works of art; rugs and tapestries, paintings and sculptures. Quality products constructed to withstand the test of time.

Restless, Ty picked up a wrench and set it down again. He had a feeling old man Fowler had hired him hoping to see him fail, though why he'd want to chance that with the venue for his daughter's wedding, Ty wasn't sure. Maybe he was wrong. If it hadn't been for the fact that this was his big chance, he would have turned the man down. And if he'd known he would be dealing directly with his past—Katy—he still would have walked.

"You ready?"

Mitch's voice drew Ty away from his vision of her last night, lost in the throes of passion. Her eyes closed and head thrown back as she rode his hand to completion.

To hell with walked, he should have run while he had a chance.

"Yeah, I'm ready."

CHAPTER NINE

Jared worked all afternoon with Larry to repair the torn ceiling and apply a new medallion in preparation for the chandelier Ty was on the hunt to replace. He'd contacted all the antique dealers he knew to try and locate a light close to the one destroyed.

From their position high up on the scaffolding they could see fresh cuts on the tarnished medal. Someone had deliberately weakened the integrity of the chandelier. Whoever had done this knew what they were doing. They'd staged it so the weight of the heavy fixture would slowly add pressure to the center pedestal until it couldn't bare the load anymore and broke.

"This don't look so good." Larry huffed, his hardhat covered head tilted at an awkward angle to better examine the damage. "Don't get me wrong, I like my job, but I never hired on to get myself killed."

"Take it easy, no one's going to die. Ty's brother will check things out. It's probably just some teenagers with time on their hands." Privately, Jared decided to see about setting up some video surveillance. So far the infractions were minor, but he wasn't anxious to get hurt on the job either.

They finished attaching the intricately carved medallion, then Jared waved Larry down first while he surveyed the room. Though old, the theatre held a charm from bygone eras hard to match in modern architecture. From his position in the concave dome, he could see across to the nearby second floor balcony. Grecian urns with chipped paint sat on raised pedestals flanking the handrails overlooking the main gallery. Three rows of torn red velvet seats stared back at him. The room's spooky atmosphere gave him the heebie-jeebies, redolent of past occupants laughing and gossiping together while waiting for the evening's entertainment to begin.

He had just turned to begin his journey down to the ground when a shadow of movement froze him in his tracks. The hair on the back of his neck lifted as though a static charge fueled the air. Jared shivered. His buddy, Frank, was the one with the supposed sixth sense, not him. He leaned over the railing and squinted into the gloom. "Who's there?"

Nothing stirred, not even a… *ghost.*

This place was getting to him. He'd never thought himself superstitious, but after his own accident—he rubbed a gloved hand over his stitches—and the stories his workmates kept blabbing on about he was rethinking his position. Between this incident and the shit with Annie… their always-complicated relationship had taken a turn for the worse since he'd found out she'd given birth to their son eight years earlier but forgot to send him the memo. And now someone had broke into her store—while she was in the building. He was losing sleep, which turned him into a larger asshole than normal, as Ty would say.

A sudden vibration shook the scaffolding.

Jared's hands white-knuckled the railing. His pulse jumped through the nearby roof. *What the…* he looked down over the edge into the laughing gaze of Larry, the moron. "Do you have a death wish, you fucking idiot?"

"Thought you could use a little shaking up." He laughed. "You should've seen your face… priceless."

"Yeah, well, when I get down from here *your* face is going to need MasterCard to restructure it, Ty or no Ty." Jared growled.

His gaze slid to the now specter-free gallery before his booted foot dropped to the first step. "Hold this thing still."

Normally he had no problem with heights. Shit, he'd performed his share of HAHO jumps without breaking a sweat, but lately... he shook his head and concentrated on making it safely to the ground.

Revenge would be sweet.

That was close.

Ramsey dropped the gun from its resting position on the back of the seat, and flopped onto his ass. His heart pounded like a freight train. His hands were clammy from the adrenaline rush.

Shit, this was fun.

The boss had warned him no injuries; it was all supposed to be made to look as if the building needed to be condemned.

"Stop the renovations. Nothing else."

But, hey, it wasn't his fault if a body or two happened to get hurt along the way. Stuff happens; sometimes it's the price of doing a job right. He grinned.

A quick glance over the chair showed a now empty scaffold. He'd better hurry up and finish before someone decided to come take a look-see. He half crawled, half crouched his way to the second last urn on the right. His hand dipped into his coat pocket and came out with a small black box. He turned it over, flipped the switch, set it inside the urn, and then made his way to the hidden hatch at the back of the room. He'd lucked out and found the door on one of his nighttime forays. It could have been a fire escape or a route for delivering liquor during the days of prohibition. Now it worked to conceal his movements.

The stairs, enclosed within the walls, were a serpentine route that led from the front to the back of the building. An underground tunnel deposited him into a root cellar about fifty feet from the back door. Perfect.

Upon entering the eight by ten room his nose pinched shut in reaction to the musty scent reminiscent of a cross between moldy potatoes and moth balls. It reminded him of his Ukrainian grandparent's farm. He'd hated that place. Hurrying across the dank cellar, sweeping away the cobwebs, he cracked the creaky wooden door open, wincing at the noise. Hard to say how long since this old building had seen any use. It was well hidden behind a thickly leaved bush, the room itself built into the side of a knoll.

He examined the surrounding area. No movement, unless you count the scrawny momma cat by the garbage bin, no doubt searching for her lost kitten. *Sorry, Mom, this is one time the cat won't come back.*

He carefully stepped out and closed the door, locking it with the rusty but sturdy lock he'd found at the secondhand store. Then he strolled away whistling. Must be lunchtime.

Katy pulled up in front of Grits and Grace and smiled at Rebecca who was waving like a lunatic from her seat at the window. She regretting not staying in touch with her old friends since moving to California. First school, then her job, and before she knew it the years had flown by. It would have served Katy right if they'd shut her out upon her return. Instead, as soon as they heard she was in town, and where she was staying, they'd gotten in touch. She hoped by inviting Rebecca and Annie to be in her wedding party she could somehow make up for her negligence.

Katy stepped from her car and gazed on the busy downtown core. Funny how she'd taken the town for granted growing up. From the family owned drug store on the corner, to the pretty flower shop, and Grace's diner; all businesses she'd been in and out of dozens of times as a child.

The sparkle of the fountain in the center of Main Street's roundabout caught her eye. She remembered when her father was on town council and lobbied for the installation of the water feature. He'd wanted to divert traffic from speeding down the road and hopefully bring more economy to the dying business district with some much needed beautification. Going by the crowd of pedestrians she saw now, he'd succeeded.

As usual, thoughts of her father left Katy conflicted. On the one hand her dad was everything a girl could ask for in a father, kind, loving, and patient—a stark contrast to their unapproachable mother. But, then there was the man, Kenneth Fowler. Him, she hadn't liked so much.

When she was sixteen Katy had overheard her brother, Kyle, arguing with their father about a planned business trip. That was the day the blinders came off. Her *kind*, *sweet* dad, was having an affair. And not for the first time apparently. Angry and embarrassed, Katy's respect all but disappeared for her father. It was only years later, that she came to understand what had driven her dad to cheat.

This wedding was a second chance for all of them to forgive, if not forget, the angry words of the past.

Returning Rebecca's wave, she locked her car and strode toward the front doors of the café. As she slipped through the sparkling glass door held open by a smiling senior, Katy inhaled the rich, dark roast aroma of freshly brewed coffee and beef barley soup. A restaurant full of gossiping customers muted the

crooning of Frank Sinatra from the old jukebox in the
corner. California was great, but it wasn't home. She'd
missed the friendly accord of neighbors laughing and
talking between tables as if they were at a social
gathering.

Rebecca stood as she neared the table, the overhead
fluorescents glinting off her raven black mane of hair.
Her periwinkle blue eyes crinkled at the edges as her
lips lifted in a mile-wide smile of greeting. "There she
is, the beautiful bride to be."

Conscious of the sudden spark of interest from
nearby tables, Katy hurried the last few steps into her
friend's warm embrace.

"I've missed you," she whispered, her throat tight
with unshed tears.

"Not half as much," Rebecca replied, then kissed her
cheek before leaning back to get a better look.
"California agrees with you."

Katy glanced down at her buttery yellow t-shirt,
distressed jeans, and open-toe sandals showing off
bright pink nails. Her hair slipped over her shoulder,
brushing her cheek. She swept it back and grinned,
shrugging. "At least it's not surfer shorts."

Rebecca giggled and returned to her seat. She lifted
her cup in a toast. "To west coast sunshine, wherever
we live." She took a sip from her steaming mug and
pointed to its twin sitting on the Formica tabletop. "I
seem to remember you being a fan of Grace's coffee,
right?"

The aroma drew a sigh of pleasure from Katy's rose
tinted lips. "Oh perfect, I've been looking forward to
this." She slid into the booth. The red leather, warm
from the sun, felt good against her back. The coffee was
hot and delicious, just as she remembered.

Fortified, she gazed around the café, noting the little
changes since her last visit. A new glass pie counter
showed off Grace's well-known talent as a pastry chef.

The black and white tiles on the floor were the same, maybe with a few more scuffmarks. The dark green walls now carried a variety of landscape paintings. There was one Katy particularly liked of the theatre with the initials S.R. written in the corner. Wonder if a local artist had done it? She'd have to ask Grace if they were for sale. It would look great on her bedroom wall back home. That is if they kept the condo after her and Jeff were married.

"It looks just the same," she sighed and sat back, cradling her cup. "I'm glad you were able to meet me. I've missed you, Becky."

Rebecca's smile turned shaky. She reached across and squeezed Katy's outstretched hand. "Me, too. I can't believe it's been so long." She turned Katy's hand over and admired the sparkling rock on her third finger. "Wow, you should have a bodyguard for that thing."

Katy pulled back with a self-conscious laugh and tucked her hand under her leg. "Jeff doesn't like to do anything small."

She glanced up and let out a little yelp of joy. "Susan, you're still here." Jumping out of the booth she gave the older woman a warm hug, inhaling hairspray and cigarette smoke mixed with a flowery perfume. The beehive hairdo scratched her cheek, or maybe that was the pen shoved behind an ear decorated with clip-on Shamrock earrings.

"Course, I am. What else would I be doing?" Susan's raspy voice grumbled as her boney fingers rubbed up and down Katy's back. "It's about damn time you came home. That boy of yours missed you awful. We all did."

The heat climbed Katy's cheeks. That *boy's* mouth had driven her crazy last night.

And his words had wrenched her heart.

She swallowed around the golf ball lodged in her throat and kissed the woman's papery cheek. "I'm sorry, Susan. I should have kept in touch. Mom sends her love."

"How is your mother? Still ruling her kingdom?" Susan tipped her head, but her beehive defied gravity and stayed upright.

Katy slid back into the booth and took another sip of the cooling coffee. "You know Mom, she's not happy unless she's making some poor schmuck miserable. I don't think she'll ever leave that hospital."

Susan barked out a laugh that turned into a coughing jag and waved away Katy's concern. "Well, it'll be good to see her next month." She glanced over the booth and a sly gleam came into her eyes. "That is if the wedding is still a go?"

Just then a big, hard body slipped into the seat beside her, almost landing in her lap. "Yeah, Katy, that's the million dollar question of the day. Is it still a go? Are you marrying your lover boy?" Ty curled his arm over the back of the booth, practically encapsulating them into their own little cocoon.

She was faintly aware of the heavy-set man Ty had arrived with sitting with Rebecca and her prickly demeanor, but the man at her side took most of Katy's attention. His woodsy scent and the warmth of his thigh touching her leg surrounded her. The mischief gleaming out of those cerulean blue eyes reminded her of the old Ty. The one who stole her heart. And then let her walk away.

She moved closer to the window, ignoring his enveloping presence. Holding out her hand—yes, the one with the boulder on it—Katy smiled at the newcomer. "Hi, I'm Katy Fowler."

The stranger grinned and clasped her hand in a beefy mitt, leaning over to bestow a kiss upon her ring. "You don't remember me? I used to chase you out of your brother's room whenever we were doing homework together."

Katy shook her head, and then all of a sudden it clicked. "That was not homework, Mitch Taylor. You guys were looking at girly pictures." She laughed, noticing Rebecca's darkening frown with curiosity. She'd have to grill her friend later.

Susan dropped the menus she'd been carrying onto the table. "I'll just let you get reacquainted," she said, and winked. "Be back to take your order in a couple of minutes." And with that she was gone, leaving an awkward silence in her wake.

Mitch slung his brawny arm around Rebecca's stiff shoulders, and ignoring her gasp, helped himself to a shot of her coffee. "Well, isn't this like a blast from the past?"

As Katy squirmed to keep a space open between her and the temptation she was sitting next to, she tried to decide whether to laugh, or groan.

CHAPTER TEN

Ty wanted to kick his own ass. What was he thinking? He'd already decided last night to put some distance between himself and the frustratingly beautiful bride-to-be. Yet the moment he'd walked into the restaurant, his senses had directed him straight to her booth like a freaking homing beacon.

Now, here he sat in the seventh level of Hell. So close he couldn't help but inhale the lavender fragrance of Katy's freshly washed hair, still slightly damp where it rested on her shoulders. So close he kept getting glimpses of the lacey edge of her white bra whenever she squirmed to avoid touching him. And the squirming... the squirming took him straight back to his kitchen the night before and his mouth feasting on her lips. Her sexy moans as his fingers teased her satiny heat and her writhing as he took her up and over the edge. The peach glow of her skin and the sultry scent of her release as she went boneless in his arms.

His jeans grew uncomfortably tight. Mitch's smug smile across the table made Ty want to kick him. Ty's addiction to Katy was no secret. Everyone in town had known. Which made it all the more important he proved he was well and truly over her.

Angry with himself and the whole situation, Ty removed his arm from the back of her seat and turned his attention to the interior of the restaurant, desperately hoping for a diversion.

His wandering gaze landed on his brother. Jack sat a few booths down and across the aisle, a sky-high platter of pancakes dripping with syrup on the table in front of him. He dipped his head in acknowledgement and gave Ty a troubled frown. Ty grimaced, and shrugged. Jack had tried to talk to him the last time Katy dumped him, but he'd been too wound up to listen. Jack was no doubt worried his brother was going to get hurt again, but Ty could have told him different. Once bitten, twice as careful; he'd learned his lesson.

Belying that, her soft laughter over something Mitch said made his stomach twist itself into a knot of jealousy. He glared across the table and Mitch smirked. Ty's scowling gaze fell on Susan serving a stranger over by the old jukebox. He caught the guy staring at their table before he turned back to his menu. Must be new in town, anyone familiar with Grits and Grace knew the list of options hardly ever varied. Grace's motto was, *"Why mess with something if it's not broken?"* Customers loved her food just the way it had been served for the past twenty years. They didn't like change. And neither did he.

But then Katy leaned forward to show something on her cell phone to her friend. The sun's rays caught in her hair and turned the gleaming strands to antique gold. He'd always loved her hair. The soft, silky, fragrant feel of it gliding over his skin. He'd been hooked from the first time he saw her, sassing him from the safety of her father's side, the flare of the flashlight highlighting her lithe figure. His gaze had followed her as she ran up the aisle, her beautiful mane flowing behind her, and just like that, he'd been lost.

Rebecca's excited shriek jolted him back to the restaurant with a start. Her hands were clasped to her chest—along with Mitch's appreciative gaze—and she vibrated with excitement.

"What did I miss?" he asked, his lips lifting with an amused quirk.

"I'm going to be a bridesmaid," she squeaked. "My first time, and it's going to be my best friend's big day. Can you believe it?" She thrust the phone into his face. "Here, look."

He had to grab it in self-defense or risk getting a black eye. Tapping the screen to refresh the picture, Ty gazed down at an undernourished model wearing a frilly dress. Not sure what he was supposed to say, all he could up with was, "Nice shade of green."

"It's sea-foam." Rebecca corrected. "And look, the hemline is cut to give a sensation of waves. Oh, and I love the model's iridescent shoes. It's perfect."

Ty was aware of Katy's unnatural stillness.

Her bated breath.

The silent waiting, as though his opinion might actually matter to her.

He met her eyes—eyes that matched the color of the dress—and answered Rebecca. "Heart-stopping."

Rebecca's soft sigh of satisfaction and Mitch's teasing all faded to white noise as a multitude of unsaid words passed between Katy's tense body and Ty's. Why was he making everything so difficult? She was getting married in six weeks. It was too late for them to be playing these old games.

But she couldn't control her body's response to his velvet dark voice or the heat in the blue-flame of his gaze. It made her dream impossible dreams. She wanted a chance to explain what happened all those years ago. To beg his forgiveness. But at the same time, she also wanted to know why he never even tried to get in touch afterward.

For months they had spent every moment together, so in love she'd known it was just a matter of time before they married. Ty was her first lover, the only one she'd ever accepted into her body. They were going to be together, have a family, and grow old together. Then it happened; her father's betrayal, her mother's depression, her brother's defection. Katy's perfect world turned upside down.

And then they were over. A few harshly said words and the supposed love of a lifetime ended.

Katy frowned as the hair stood up on the back of her neck. Someone was staring at her. She searched the vicinity of the restaurant, not quite sure whether it was her imagination or not. Her gaze landed on a stranger sitting by the jukebox. His dark head was down perusing a newspaper spread out across the table. She squinted to make out the tattoo on the back of the hand holding the page. Shrugging, she gave up and moved on to the next table.

Now, there was a man she knew.

"Ty," Katy turned, her voice pitching upward in excitement. "Ty, your brother is here." She squeezed his arm, temporarily setting their differences aside. "When did Jack become sheriff?"

The muscles under her hand had tightened to steel. "What's wrong?"

Ty's attention seemed to be focused on the man sitting behind his brother. "Nothing's wrong. He's been sheriff for a couple of years now."

His shoulders seemed to grow wider, boxing her into her corner of the booth. "Do you know that guy?"

She took a second look. "I don't think so, why?"

"He just seems familiar, that's all." Ty turned to gaze down at her, concern lighting the depths of his eyes. "You need to be careful. This isn't the quiet little town you grew up in anymore. We get our share of transients."

Katy couldn't help the burst of laugher. "You do realize I live in LA, right?"

Ty's eyebrows pulled down. "That's right, city girl, laugh it up. It won't be so funny when some jerk manages to sneak up on you because you figure you're invincible. The craft store down the street was broken into a few days ago. You need to pay attention, that's all I'm trying to say."

Katy ignored the 'city girl' remark in favor of the warm glow washing over her from his concern. He'd masked it with gruffness, but she saw the worry etched along his tightened jaw and lowered brows. Even though she didn't necessarily agree with him—in comparison to LA, Tidal Falls was as safe as a Sunday church service—she would do as he asked. It was better to be safe than sorry.

"He's right, Katy. Annie told me all about it. She said he threw a knife and it just missed her." Rebecca leaned over the table and stage-whispered the news. "It landed in the mannequin she uses for sewing class. She's pretty upset."

"Seriously? That is scary. Why would anyone break into a craft store?" Katy turned to the man at her side. "I'm sorry, Ty. I promise to be careful, okay?"

He gazed down at her as if he wanted to say more, then bit his tongue. "Okay."

Ramsey kept his eyes down, staring at the paper laid out in front of him without reading a single word. On a scale of one to ten, this was a solid seven in the bad idea department. First the damn cop had to go and sit in the booth right in front of him. Then Reno boy had to go and turn suspicious like. He wasn't too worried, even if they did decide to question him, this po-dunk police force probably wouldn't have a clue.

On the other hand, if they did a background search it wouldn't turn out well for him. Better he just keep his head down, and nose clean. Prison food sucked. With the money from this job, he could disappear for a while. Rent a condo on a beach, maybe somewhere like Barbados. Entertain a hot babe or two. Yeah, he could see it now. All he had to do was stop the renovation of the theatre and the cash was his.

And if he got the chance to have some fun with little Miss Sunshine while he was at it, all the better.

CHAPTER ELEVEN

What was it about Katy Fowler that made him feel like an over-sexed teenager? Even as he drew plans on a napkin and discussed the feasibility of what he wanted to get done with Mitch, Ty's attention remained focused on the woman at his side.

She precisely measured half a teaspoon of sugar to pour into her coffee, then ripped open two little creamers before carefully stirring the concoction together. His hungry gaze followed her hand as it brought the ceramic cup to temptingly puckered lips parted to blow lightly across the surface of the liquid. Her intent might be to cool, but instead it drove his temperature into the stratosphere.

Ty prided himself on his normally responsible attitude. His two older sisters, one a psychologist and the other a lawyer, and his superhero brother, Jack, babied him. He had to work hard to prove his independence to them. And now, just when he was making something of his life—reaching some measure of success—Katy hurtled back into his life like a meteor on a collision course, and ripped his comfortable world apart.

The rest of lunch at Grace's was uneventful. Katy and Rebecca talked wedding plans over plates of fancy looking salads while Ty worked out the details of the afternoon's welding job with Mitch. It almost had the feel of a double date, which should have had him running for the hills, but didn't.

"So, what are you thinking?" Mitch repeated, tapping his fork against the side of his plate to get Ty's attention.

Ty finished drawing the final lines on his paper diagram and gave the napkin a twist so his friend could see it better. "I'm *thinking* I want the stage to be in two sections. The back will be stationary, but the front will have three distinct levels." He pointed to the sidebar where he'd roughly drawn what he meant. "There's a stage level for big performances, floor level for more intimate shows, and the dropped level for orchestras during plays and recitals."

"Is that really necessary?" Mitch asked skeptically.

No, it probably wasn't, but it's what Ty wanted, and since he'd been given carte blanche...

Katy, overhearing their conversation, leaned closer to get a better look, and her hair brushed his forearm resting on the table. The slight contact sent a shiver of want straight to his groin. He cleared his suddenly parched throat and reached for the water glass.

"This looks amazing. Are you going to have the time to get it finished?" She turned those cat's eyes onto him and blinked.

No, he wasn't sure they could get it done in time, but he was going to give it his best shot. It was a matter of pride now. "Don't you have any faith in me, sugar?"

A flush crept up her neck and she leaned back in her seat. "I never said that, it was an honest question." And then, as if he didn't feel like a big enough asshole, she added, "Tidal Falls is lucky to have you. This will make a big difference to the performing arts for the town. Thank you."

Well, shit.

Kind of hard to retain an attitude against that, she took the wind out of his sails every damn time. Ignoring their audience across the table, he grasped her hand in a light squeeze and then pulled his plans over so she could have a better look.

"Want to see how this is going to work?"

Katy sat up, relieved that the mini crisis had been averted. She hadn't meant to ridicule Ty's work ethic, anything but. He'd come a long way from the young man she'd given her heart to as a teen. It was obvious that his employees respected him, and more than that, they liked him. Not an easy thing when you're a boss. Ask her mother.

Pointing at a top portion of the hand-drawn stage she asked, "What's this for?"

Ty used his carpenter's pencil to shade the area in to look like heavy drapery. "That's called the proscenium archway. It's meant to create a frame around the performers so that the audience's attention stays front and center. It also helps to hide what's happening in the wings."

Katy nodded. She'd seen stages like this before, but never realized the significance of the arrangement. "How do the curtain thingy's work?"

Ty grinned. "Do you mean the pulleys?"

She shrugged, enjoying his enthusiasm.

"There are two ways they can open and close. One is called the guillotine style where the front curtain ascends straight up, or down. The other is named the travelers, which means they can move to the side, travelling across the stage. Make sense?"

"So far, yes." She glanced at him quizzically. "What about for screen productions though? Are we still going to be able to show movies?"

Ty nodded. He flipped the napkin over and drew a few quick slashes near the top. Suddenly, she could see a raised catwalk with lights and pulleys.

"This is what's known as the fly gallery. From here props, sets, even screens can be lowered on the fly, providing whatever is needed for the production. So for movies we can lower the screen, set up a projector, and there you have it, a theatre is born."

He looked so proud of his ideas. Katy couldn't help her response. She clapped, softly at first, and then when Rebecca chimed in, loud enough costumers turned to look. And still she clapped. Ty's ears reddened and he reached out and grabbed her hands, stopping her.

"Enough already. What are you doing?" He frowned across the table as Mitch snorted into his coffee cup. "Watch it, wise guy, you're next." Then he leaned over and whispered in her ear, his warm breath sending a shiver down her spine. "You should get spanked for that."

Holy.

Moly.

The man was lethal. He should come with a warning label: Danger of exploding hormones if within radius of erogenous zones.

Katy sat in a sensual fog as Mitch and Ty gathered the sketched plans, finished coffee, and paid the bill for lunch. After a hurried goodbye, they left the restaurant to get back to work. Rebecca's soft laughter brought her down to earth, the cacophony of a crazy lunch rush jarring her sensitized nerves.

"What's so funny?"

"You are. You're still into him, aren't you?" Rebecca's sympathetic eyes made Katy feel twitchy.

"Of course not. Ty and I were over long ago, you know that." Even as the words tripped over themselves leaving her lips, Katy's gaze followed his broad back outside as he made his way over to his truck. She'd always liked his walk. He strode with confidence, those long legs eating up the distance.

"Katy…" her friend's worried voice drew her eyes reluctantly away from the windowpane.

"What?" She picked up her spoon and absently stirred the rapidly cooling coffee.

"If you're not sure…"

"*I am.*" Katy interrupted, but couldn't quite meet Rebecca's gaze. "Jeff's perfect for me. He'll be here soon enough, and then you'll see."

Rebecca held her hand up in a stop motion. "Hey, you don't need to convince me, I'm on your side, okay." She lowered her hand to slow the twirling spoon. "I just don't want you to do something you might later regret, that's all. Take it from the voice of experience, some mistakes are hard to reverse."

What had she missed in Rebecca's life while she'd been gone? Katy was about to ask what brought those shadows to her friend's expressive eyes when Ty's brother stopped at their table.

"Ladies." He tapped the brim of his Stetson. "Your pretty faces just made my day a little bit brighter."

Katy smiled. She'd always liked Ty's family. "Jack, Ty was just telling me you were a sheriff now, congratulations. How's the rest of your family?"

"They're good, busy, but good. Mind if I join you for a moment?" Jack slid into Ty's seat, his bulky shoulders taking up most of the free space. "So, you're getting married, huh?"

Katy shared an arched eyebrow with Rebecca at his more than obvious fishing expedition. "Well, that's the word on the street," she replied.

He shook his head, "Caught out, am I? You can't fault a guy for watching out for his kid brother, now can you?"

No, she understood the need to protect those you loved, probably better than anyone. So instead of telling him to mind his own business. Katy stretched her arms around his considerable bulk and gave him an awkward hug.

"You're a good man, Jack Garrett. Ty is safe from my lecherous hands. I don't have any designs on his admittedly fine physique. Is that what you're waiting to hear?"

Liar, Liar.

Even as she sat back and smiled the smile of the innocent, Katy childishly crossed her fingers at the fib. She didn't *want* to get mixed up with Ty again, unfortunately her heart seemed to have different plans.

Jack's attention wandered to the stranger she'd noticed earlier. He stood at the till now, his back to the table. The newspaper he'd been reading was rolled up and tucked under his arm revealing what looked like a holster under the edge of the man's jacket.

Her heart beat faster. Why would a passerby need a gun?

Obviously the sheriff wanted an answer to that question also because he sent a distracted smile their way as he rose from the table, ready to follow the male out the door. "I'm glad everything worked out for you, Katybug. I'll see you before the big day, I'm sure." He tipped his hat at Rebecca, "Ladies." Then he was gone, a man on a mission.

"Well, that was strange." Rebecca said, peering out the window to see if she could catch the action.

Katy couldn't agree more. She hoped Jack knew what he was doing. She'd never agreed with the concept of *'open carry'* for firearms. To her that just asked for trouble. Katy was firmly on the make love, not war side of the gun debate. How can the law be expected to adequately police the people when every Joe on the street over the age of majority could legally carry a weapon? She'd seen firsthand the effects of a bullet versus a human body; the result wasn't pretty, and could potentially be deadly. That last thought had her searching up and down the block. Ty hadn't left all that long ago, she hoped he didn't get caught in the middle of something he wasn't trained to handle. Like a freaking gunfight for example.

Suddenly too anxious to sit still, Katy slid out of the booth.

"What are you doing?" Rebecca hissed, her voice teeming with undercurrents of excitement and worry.

Katy pasted a reassuring smile on her face. "Just going to the washroom, I'll be right back. See if Susan will give us one more refill, okay?" Then, without waiting for a reply, Katy hurried down the aisle, but instead of taking a right toward the washrooms, she went left into the kitchen.

Grace, busy at a sizzling grill filled with the tantalizing aroma of frying onions and bacon, never even looked around. But over the noise of the dishwasher, a young man in a snowy white apron, his hair a mass of tight dark curls, made a move as if to usher her to the front. Katy lifted a forefinger to her lips and slipped past the bemused teen to slide out the back door. The alley, in contrast to the racket of the restaurant, was eerily silent.

Katy stepped down off the cement landing onto the gravel drive. The shadows created by the neighboring building brought goose bumps skittering across the surface of her skin. Maybe this wasn't a good idea. But she couldn't just sit there as if nothing was going on. And besides, if anyone did get hurt—pray God not—it would be better if she was on scene when it happened.

Pulling up her courage, Katy edged her way along the side of the building toward the garbage dumpster. She jumped once when a stray cat suddenly hissed before hopping the fence across the alley and disappearing from sight. No gunshots yet, that was reassuring at least. When she reached the bin, Katy peeked around the side, saw the cars cruising back and forth on the street in front of the café, and decided everything must be okay.

She straightened, dusted down her dress, and hurried toward the patch of sunlight, which seemed to represent safety from the dank alley. Just as she cleared the front of the dumpster she caught a movement out of the corner of her eye. Before she could do much more than suck in a sharp inhale, a steely arm wrapped around her throat and dragged her back to the shadows.

CHAPTER TWELVE

Kyle Fowler knew all the scientific studies conducted over the years about the psychic abilities of twins. Some said the connection was coincidental, while others believed it to be more spiritual or intuition. He didn't normally buy into the whole hocus pocus, ESP nonsense, but he did know whenever his sister was in some kind of distress. Now was definitely one of those times. His guts were killing him. She'd been on his mind the whole day, up to and including his date with the oh-so-desirable Penny Lee. Surprising how hard it is to lock lips with a woman when all you can see is your sister's hurt eyes staring back at you.

Annoyed, and more than a little worried, Kyle dropped his disappointed date off at her home and hurried back to the base. He opened his laptop and waited for the connection to home, fingers tapping an impatient beat on the edge of the table. He enjoyed many things about Vicenza, Italy, but Internet service wasn't one of them. His thoughts circled around his dysfunctional family much like the loading icon twirling on the screen.

He'd never forget arriving home early from school and catching his father screwing the cleaning lady. His dad swore it was a mistake and he'd never do it again. Yeah, right. Until the next time, and the time after that.

The worst of it was, Kyle had known and couldn't say anything, because he didn't want to hurt his mother or sister.

The guilt became a heavy burden made worse because Katy sensed something was wrong and demanded answers he couldn't give. It all came to a head just before his eighteenth birthday. His father, the man Kyle had idolized since boyhood, made a pass at his then girlfriend and he lost his temper. Words said in the heat of anger couldn't easily be forgotten. But even worse, when Kyle turned to stomp out of the house, his mom stood in the front entry, her eyes huge with shock.

Not long after, their happy family disintegrated. Mom and Katy moved to California, while he went looking to get drunk and ended up in the army. He didn't know, and told himself he didn't care, what happened to his father.

Funny he should think of that now, while waiting to hear from home. Kyle shifted on the wooden chair in his cramped kitchenette. He'd lucked into this little ground floor apartment when he first arrived in Vicenza. He liked his privacy when off-duty and single accommodations here were at a premium. The size of the place didn't bother him, he mostly only came home to sleep anyway. However, the annoying upstairs neighbor certainly did. Kyle had yet to meet whomever lived there, but if they insisted on doing acrobatics or whatever it was they were up to at three in the morning, he was going to have to lodge a complaint.

And cue the country music.

Kyle grimaced. He didn't mind a little Johnny Cash or Waylon Jennings once in a while—a long while— but the new age crap playing now barely qualified as music, much less country.

He'd just set his hands on the table in preparation of pushing up from his seat to grab the nearby broom handle he saved for these occasions when the message on the screen went from, *please wait a moment, to now connecting.*

Instant anxiety placed a chokehold on his throat. His mother's face filled the screen in 3-D, and Kyle was guiltily grateful his sister had been the one to sacrifice her youth to supporting her after the split rather than him. Their mother, a perfectionist and reserved with her affections, had fallen apart after her husband's infidelity.

Kyle sat back, vainly trying to act nonchalant in front of his mom's eagle eyes. "Hi, Mom, how's it hanging?" She hated when he used colloquialisms like that, which is why he did it of course.

As expected, her pencil-lined brows drew together in a sign of disapproval. "Kyle. Why aren't you off saving the world? That's your usual excuse for never calling home, isn't it?"

Yep, same old mom. "That's true, Mom. It takes a lot of work to become a superhero, you know."

"Oh, Kyle," a mother's sigh of 'aren't you ever going to grow up?' ripened her haughty voice, before her eyes softened with concern. "How are you, son?"

His leg jiggled nervously and he had a hard time meeting her gaze. "I'm good, I'm in Italy, what could be wrong?" An uncomfortable silence filled the room, almost stifling the country twang from upstairs. Kyle cleared his throat. "How are the wedding plans coming along?"

She fiddled with the string of iridescent pearls around her neck. "So far as I know everything is going according to what her father wants. I don't know why she couldn't get married here. Her fiancé, Jeff, promised her any venue she desired, but you know your sister, she loves that old theatre."

Yeah, Kyle did too. There was a special feel to the building, like a favorite, slightly threadbare shirt you just can't quite part with. He and Katy had spent a good portion of their younger years running up and down those red-carpeted aisles between shows. He remembered the excitement of the projection room; the pride shining from his dad's green eyes as he watched his son learn the business. Good memories were tied up in the old girl. He was glad it was getting restored for the wedding.

"That's actually what I was calling about, Mom. Have you heard from Katy recently?" Kyle leaned closer to the screen. For some reason his body tensed, as though preparing for a blow but not sure where it was going to land. His heart picked up speed and his hands turned sweaty.

Fiona frowned in concentration, tapping a manicured finger against her jawline. "No, and now that I think about it, she was supposed to call me yesterday about the flowers." She shook her head and clicked her tongue, "I warned her going back there was a bad idea. She has a good life here with Jeff and the hospital. Why go and muddy that up with the past? What's over is over, we've all moved on."

Kyle ignored his mother's dissention and cut to the part that interested him. "So she's gone back home to make sure everything is Katy perfect?"

She frowned at his words, though her forehead stayed suspiciously smooth. "I believe that's what I just said, yes. There was no need. We could have handled everything just fine from here."

"Don't worry, Mom. She's probably just caught up with the renovations and forgot. Give her a day or two, I'm sure she'll get back to you." He made a show of looking at his watch. "Listen, Mom, I've gotta go. I'll see you in a couple of weeks. I have to come home in time to get fitted for my monkey suit."

"Kyle, I hardly think a twenty-five hundred dollar outfit qualifies as a *monkey suit*." Fiona straightened her own custom-fitted jacket, and then sent him a laser-eyed glance. "You make sure you tell me if your sister is in trouble. See you soon." And with those cryptic words she clicked off their connection.

Kyle slowly leaned back and let out a bark of laughter, frowning when the neighbor stomped on the floor in protest. There was no pulling the wool over his momma's eyes. Guess his next move was to apply for early leave. He'd better go to Tidal Falls himself and make sure all was as it should be. Again his gut gave that little warning twist.

A hand reeking of newsprint and coffee covered Katy's nose and mouth and stopped her frightened scream.

Her ankle turned painfully as she was dragged backward into the dimness of the alley. Her heart pounded through her veins and in her ears until it was all she could hear. There was barely room above the human gag to draw breath and her vision began to darken around the edges. Her captor, sensing her impending blackout, eased the pressure enough to let in a draft of much-needed cool air past her muffled sounds of distress.

Fear threatened to overwhelm her but she needed to keep her wits if she wanted to get out of this unharmed. The body, flush against her back, felt compact and strong. The man's forearm tightened as he leaned in and snarled close to her ear.

"Keep quiet, or I'll shut you up. Understand?" His breath stunk of garlic and cigarettes as he forced her head back against his shoulder, keeping her off-balance and at his mercy.

Katy whimpered, more scared than she'd ever been in her life. She was officially too stupid to live. Her panicked gaze flickered sideways and verified what she'd already guessed; it was the stranger from the restaurant. What did he want? Where was Jack? Hard on the heels of those thoughts came the vision of Ty striding to his pick-up. God, please let him be long gone from here.

"You thought you was a smart one, didn't ya?" He snickered and rubbed his bristly chin against her forehead, causing hives to break out all over her skin. "Thought you could sneak up on ol' Ramsey, did you now?"

"What do you want?" Katy mumbled the words around the sausage-like appendages holding her hostage.

"Shh," he hissed, forcing her back around the edge of the dumpster as two teens went laughing by on the sidewalk out front with not a worry in the world. "We don't want the sheriff showing up to mess with our fun, now do we?"

He kept his eyes focused on the movement going by on the street even as the deadweight that was his arm settled across the tops of Katy's heaving breasts, pinning her against his muscular torso.

"Let me go, please. I promise I won't say a word to anyone," Katy begged, hoping her assailant would listen. Why, oh, why hadn't she stayed within the safe confines of the restaurant and let Jack do his job? The one he was trained for, and she most definitely was not.

"You don't mean that, darlin', you and I are going to have a mighty fine time just as soon as things quiet down a wee bit. Though adrenaline works wonders on Petey here," he grinned as he ground his crotch against her bum.

God, help me. Please.

As if in answer to her silent plea, the screen on the café banged back on its hinges and Grace came trundling out the door lugging an armload of cardboard boxes with the dishwasher kid close behind carrying a couple of hefty garbage bags.

There was a moment of complete silence, and then all hell broke loose. Grace let out a war whoop and came flying off the back stair like a crazed banshee, while the teen dropped the bags and grabbed a nearby corn broom. He raised it over his curly head like a batter about to nail a homer and followed right behind Grace.

The noise caught the attention of people on the street. They pointed and ran towards them shouting for the sheriff. Realizing his chance for a clean escape was rapidly narrowing her captor loosened his hold and with a rough shove between the shoulder blades, sent Katy hurtling in Grace's direction. The last thing she heard before she fainted was his taunting voice.

"Watch your back, bitch. I'm coming for you."

CHAPTER THIRTEEN

Katy slowly regained consciousness. Her eyelids fluttering at the voice coming from above her head, harsh and strained with intense emotion.

"Stand back. Everyone just give her a little room." His gruff tone warned people away.

After a brief start she settled into the safety of Ty's gentle arms.

"What the hell happened?"

She almost smiled at the vexed anger she just knew would be flashing like lightning from the depths of his eyes. He'd always told her if patience were a virtue, he'd missed out on his fair share. It felt nice laying here, cradled in his arms. That is until the scene in the alley came racing back, and almost threw her into an all-new panic attack.

A feather light peck on the tip of her nose accompanied by his softly intimate words calmed her down. "Come on, Sleeping Beauty. A prince's kiss awakens the damsel in distress, remember?"

Oh, she remembered. Katy had loved the fairytale as a child, and later as a teen. She'd dragged Ty to see the movie when it was re-mastered and he'd claimed it as their story, with her mother cast as the evil queen who had never approved of their dating.

Her eyes slowly opened onto his worried gaze. The irises were almost cobalt with a ring of blue fire around them. "Hi," she whispered, loath to break the spell.

"You scared the shit out of me. Next time you want to take a nap, wait until you get home, okay?" Relief flashed across his face and his sexy dimple made an appearance. He glanced up, and that's when she realized they were surrounded by curious onlookers.

Embarrassed, Katy struggled to lift up out of Ty's arms, but he wasn't letting go. "Thank you, but I'm fine now," she said with stilted dignity.

"Relax, Doc. As you should know, when you've had a shock you need to rest for a bit." Ty full out smiled, obviously reassured that she was awake now and uninjured. "Besides, I kinda like hanging out in alleys."

"Are you okay, honey?" Grace leaned in to get a better look. "I swear, what's this town coming to? A person isn't even safe to walk outside anymore."

Katy had heard of Grace's run-in with some very bad men last spring and felt horrible for upsetting her again. "This was my own fault, Grace. I should have stayed inside with Rebecca, instead of playing amateur detective." She lifted a shaking hand, and Grace's pudgy fingers clamped on. "Thanks for being there. Without you and your helper, I don't know what would have happened." A violent aftershock ran through her body, and Ty hugged her closer.

"Where *is* my brother anyway?" he asked, and heads swiveled, searching for the missing sheriff.

Rebecca pushed through the growing crowd and fell to her knees beside them. She gaped at the bruises already forming on Katy's cheek and neck. Tears threatened but she impatiently brushed them away with trembling fingers. "That figures," she said with forced gaiety, "only back for a couple of days and you already have half the town at your feet."

Katy forced a smile through her still tender lips, and this time when she tried, Ty let her sit up, though he kept a protective arm wrapped around her back for support.

"You know me, Becky, I need to be the life of the party." She leaned over and gave her friend a swift hug. "Don't cry I'm fine." Then she whispered, "Help me get out of here, okay?"

Rebecca gave her a grave look before glancing over her shoulder at Ty. "You should get her to a doctor for a check-up. Make sure that asshole didn't hurt my girl."

Katy grimaced. That wasn't exactly what she meant. "Don't worry about it, Ty. I can get myself to the clinic. If I thought I needed to, which I don't." She ignored her aches and pains and scrambled to her feet. "See, all's good."

She turned as Ty rose to tower behind her. "You're supposed to be at work anyway, right? I don't want to hold you up." He stiffened and she realized how her words could be construed. "Ty, that's not…"

The pop, pop of firearms discharging echoed into the alley. Ty grabbed her, pushing her down and under his body. "Take cover," he yelled, his voice rumbling through her thumping chest.

She wrapped her arms around his back and tugged, begging him to make a smaller target of himself. He ignored her, keeping most of his weight off her slighter form while acting as human body armor. His eyes pierced the shadows in search of the source of the shots. Then he turned the intensity of his gaze onto her and Katy's breath caught in her throat.

Their history together and all they had meant to each other played like a kaleidoscope within those burning blue depths. What happened to them? Why didn't she fight harder to stay with him? Why didn't he fight to keep her? So many questions. Would they ever get a chance to answer them?

She sucked in a harsh breath and her breasts brushed against his chest. They both froze. Katy broke eye contact first, turning her head to stare at the dumpster she'd been pinned against not very long ago. *That's all this is, adrenaline.* They'd had their chance years ago. *It's too late for regrets now.*

"I think it's over." Ty's words on the heels of her thoughts brought tears to the surface. Then she realized he meant the standoff.

"Yeah, I think so too," she said, and if her voice was somewhat wobbly, Katy hoped it would be attributed to the gunman. "Do you suppose it was the man who grabbed me?"

"I'm not sure." He lifted up in one smooth motion and a rush of cool air chilled her lonely body. Ty eyed the small crowd, before reaching down to pull her to her feet. "Stay here. And this time I mean it. I'm just going to check on Jack."

His mouth was grim as he looked down into her upturned face. "This is what I was talking about, or do you think you brought some L.A. excitement back with you?" Then he dropped a quick kiss on her mouth, and was gone.

Katy stared stupidly after him for a moment before giving her head a shake and hurrying over to help Grace who had fallen to her knees at the sound of the gunfire and now had trouble getting up.

"Grace, are you injured?" she placed her arm around the older woman's waist and helped her to her feet with the young teen's help.

"Of course not. It'd take more than some idiot playing *Gunsmoke* to keep this old girl down." She brushed trembling fingers down her apron front before grasping Katy's forearm. "It's you I'm worried about. Did that lunatic hurt you?"

"No, thanks to both of you, he never got the chance. I feel like an idiot."

Grace looked at her in astonishment. "For what, child? Caring about your friends? There's nothing to be ashamed about in that, is there, Teddy?"

The young man blushed, his gaze dropping to the scuffed toes of his high-tops. "No, ma'am, and it's Ted… ma'am," he mumbled.

"Well, that's what I said, didn't I?" Grace grumbled. "C'mon, we better get back inside. We have customers waiting on their food."

The crowd had begun an exodus back to the street. Katy joined Rebecca following behind Grace. She heard her name called and lifted onto her toes to see past the people in front of them. Mitch waved wildly from the front of the group.

"Hurry, it's Doc Johnson. He's been hit."

Run, Run, fast as you can, you can't catch me, I'm the invisible man.

Where could he go?

Hurry, gotta hide.

Ramsey slowed his pace, glancing nervously over his shoulder. No one yet. He edged up to the rusty wire fence, half expecting Cujo to jump out from the dimness between the rows of piled up scrap metal.

Nothing, it was his lucky day.

He snickered aloud. A close call this morning, followed by a near catch of his prize—the woman—then a bit of target practice, and now a nice jog through town. A good day so far.

Ramsey sucked in a deep breath of oil and grease fumes and climbed the barrier, dropping to the other side on cat's feet. He crouched there for a moment, and when nothing moved, scurried into the auto parts graveyard. Bellying into an old Cadillac Coupe Deville's still luxurious backseat, Ramsey lay still and watched the dust motes float through the air. He was ninety-five percent certain he'd lost the cop a couple streets back, but better to play it safe for a while. Maybe catch an afternoon nap. Contemplate his next move.

He might have trouble outdoing today's little adventure. A smirk twisted his unremarkable face. She'd just about shit her pants when he grabbed her. That frail heart had pounded so hard Ramsey thought he might have to give her some mouth to mouth. He shifted, then stilled when the leather creaked out a warning. Yeah, he'd like to give her a little resuscitation, all right. Soon. Soon it would be just the two of them.

Then the fun could really begin.

As Ty worked to stop the flow of blood from Doc Johnson's thigh, the warm copper scent filled his mouth and nose until he thought he would drown from it. Faintly surprised how dark a red it was, he kept up the count in his head.

One, two, three.

Ease up.

One, two, three.

There was so much of the viscous, life-draining, plasma leaking out from between his fingers. He couldn't stem the flow. He tried. He *Goddamn* tried, but it just wouldn't stop.

And then, suddenly it did.

He couldn't look into Doc's graying face, so he just kept counting. One, two, three. One, two…

"He's gone, Ty." Someone, Katy, leaned over and gently shut Doc's eyes with shaking fingers. Funny that, Doc taking care of Doc. "You did everything you could. C'mon, Ty, let him go."

He had to force himself to release the bloody leg. A pool of liquid congealed around the body and roiled in his gut. Suddenly, he was violently angry. So angry his whole frame shuddered with the force of it.

Katy tried to wrap her arms around his shoulders, but he shook her off, growling, "No. I'm not the one in need of comfort."

He rose to his feet in a controlled rush, stained hands raised in a plea. "How am I supposed to tell Doc's wife he's not coming home ever again? His kids, fuck, his grandkids."

Ty turned away, and then swung back, a giant ball of pain twisting his gut into a knot of desolation. "Christ, Katy, I just said hello to him a few minutes ago. How could this have happened?"

Tears ran down Katy's pale face and dripped off her chin. "I don't know. Maybe if I hadn't gotten in the way, Jack would have caught the guy before any of this happened. I just don't know."

Jack. Where was his brother?

Ty turned a frantic gaze on the now silent crowd that had formed around the trio. Most lowered their eyes, afraid to make contact with the raw agony no doubt shining from his. Mitch stood to one side with Rebecca tucked into his chest sobbing. Grace had her arms around the young dishwasher and Annie Campbell.

Jack broke through the throng and came to a sliding halt.

His chest heaved and sweat ran freely down his flushed face. Ty took a running tally of his brother's body, before releasing a sigh of relief. They might not see eye-to-eye most of the time, but they were family.

Jack's somber gaze took in everything in an instant. Doc's figure, Ty's stiffening red hands, the crying women, and came to the correct conclusion, "He's dead?"

Ty nodded, "Femoral artery. There nothing I could do, he bled out."

Jack rubbed a tired hand across the back of his neck. "The son-of-a-bitch opened fire as soon as he saw me. I chased him all over town, but he got away." He glanced at Katy. "How's she holding up? Their families were pretty close."

Yeah, Ty grimaced. He remembered. "I have to talk to you." He motioned to the crowd. "Private."

Jack checked his watch. "It's going to have to wait. I need to process the scene, get an APB out on the suspect, and question the witnesses." He dug his phone out of his pocket. "Listen, why don't you take her home and I'll stop by later to get your statements. She needs to decompress, you both do." Almost before he finished speaking, Jack had turned away with his phone to his ear calling in reinforcements.

Ty frowned after his brother, then moved to Katy's side. "C'mon, I'm getting outta here."

"What about our statements?" Katy swayed, and caught herself on his forearm.

"Jack said he'd drop by later. Let's get you out of here before he changes his mind."

As they moved past the body the ambulance arrived, followed by the coroner's van and a couple of police cars. At least Jack would have some assistance now.

"Where do you think he is?" her voice quivered.

"In the next state, if he knows what's good for him," Ty said. He stretched over the side of the pick-up for a rag. "Get in, I'll be right there."

He rubbed his hands almost raw before tossing the rag into a nearby garbage can. He couldn't wait to get home and wash the horror of the day's events away. Preferably not alone, but he knew that was a pipedream. It wouldn't be fair to use their past history together for sex anyway. And that wasn't even counting the fact she was engaged and strictly out of bounds.

He opened the driver's door and frowned. Katy sat huddled in the corner, her sunflower hair wilting, great green eyes bubbling over with tears, and shoulders shaking from shock. It pissed him off all over again to see the marks her would-be abductor had left on her creamy skin. If he ever caught up to the fucker, Ty would be happy to show him how a real man fights.

He stretched over the front seat and grabbed Tiger's blanket from the back. "Here, wrap up before you catch a chill." She looked small and lost covered up in the old gray army quilt. Now he had two stray females to look after. His life was getting complicated.

Ty started the truck and directed warm air her way before pulling away from the crime scene. He caught her gazing into the side mirror and sought to distract her attention.

"So what's up between Mitch and Rebecca?"

Lame, Garrett.

He shot her a swift sideways glance. Sure enough, she was staring at him as if he'd lost his marbles.

"How the heck should I know? A good man dies today, and you want to talk about *romance?*" Katy's voice shot up an octave, and she threw the blanket off in a fit of annoyance. "Are you serious?"

Ty slapped a palm on the steering wheel and then swore under his breath when he saw her jump nervously. "No, I'm not freaking serious." His voice rang with frustrated anger. "What *I am*..." he gritted past clenched teeth, but the spooked look that entered her eyes told him clearer than any words to calm the hell down.

He blew out a long breath and started again, "What I am is pissed at myself for leaving the restaurant ahead of you in the first place. If I'd manned up and gotten my stupid libido under control, this never would have happened."

"It wasn't our fault Doc was shot, Ty. I feel as guilty as you do... guiltier even. But we weren't the ones to pull the trigger." Katy tucked the blanket up to her chin.

There was a strained silence after that for the time it took him to drive home. He turned the corner onto his street and pulled up to the house before chancing her another glance.

She was smiling. The little vixen.

He turned off the key and rested his arm across the top of the steering wheel. "What's so funny?"

"Us." She pulled a slim hand—the one with the eye-piercingly bright diamond—out from the folds of the blanket and smoothed a hank of hair behind her ear. "We always do this." When he stared at her in puzzlement, she dropped her hand to her lap and fiddled with the woven edge of the material before continuing. "We try so hard to protect each other that we end up pushing us apart instead."

Yeah, she was probably right, but that didn't change anything. He needed to take care of her; it was hard-wired into his system. He had no choice. And before he started thinking about what *that* meant, he was going for a much-needed shower.

"Look, I'm not really up to a philosophical discussion. Let's shelve this for now, okay?" He opened his door, climbed out, and went around to her side. Then waited until she jumped down before adding, "It's not bad to care about each other, you know. Just because we couldn't work things out between us, doesn't mean the feelings shut off like a water tap. They don't... didn't, I mean."

Then, before he could get himself into more trouble, Ty gathered her up into his arms and helped her into what once was to be their dream home.

CHAPTER FOURTEEN

By the time Jack processed the scene, broke the tragic news to Doc Johnson's widow and wrote up page-after-blinking-page of reports, he was tired, depressed, and ready for a beer or three. Unfortunately he still needed to drop by his brother's house and pick up his daughter from her job at The Craft Shack.

That was another issue he had to deal with. Even though it was no doubt a one-off, never to happen again occurrence, Jack didn't want his baby girl working at the shop after the break-in. They'd argued about it this morning, not that that was anything new. Ever since puberty hit, an alien seemed to have inhabited his daughter's body. One with big teeth. Jack never knew when he might get his head snapped off. Before that, he'd thought dealing with criminals was stressful.

The phone rang just as he finished straightening his files into neat orderly rows on the corner of his walnut desk. It rang again, and again. He swore and glared daggers through the closed door of his office. What was the sense of having a secretary if she couldn't even answer the phones?

He heaved a tension-releasing breath and picked up the receiver. "Chief Garrett's office, how can I help you?"

"Daddy?"

Jack smiled and relaxed, leaning back in his chair, and relieved the monster occupying his daughter's body seemed to be sleeping for the moment.

"Tina. I was just thinking about coming to pick you up. Did you and Annie," his heart pinged with regret, "get everything put back together okay?"

He'd enjoyed his dates with Annie the past couple of months. They had fun together. But he wasn't blind. Now that Jared Martin had returned to town, Jack could see the writing on the wall. The two of them had a past they needed to get sorted. And he had Tina.

"Almost. I told you she would need a hand. We've worked our butts off all day." There was a small I-need-courage-so-I-can-ask pause, "Dad…"

Uh, oh here it comes. He could almost feel the monster's flames already. "Just spit it out, it's easier that way."

"Daddy." Tina puffed out an annoyed breath.

"I know you're probably going to say no, but Ted asked me to go for dinner with him," she said in a rush of syllables, as if hoping the going out on a *date* thing would slide right by him.

Not. In. A. Million. Freaking. Years.

She was going to be the death of him, he just knew it. The gray was popping into his receding hairline as she spoke. "Ted, who?" he asked in what he thought was a fairly reasonable tone of voice. Considering.

Tina sighed the sigh of beleaguered teens everywhere. "Seriously? You know Ted, Dad. His father owns Duke's, Mr. Farley?" She said, using a virtual cattle prod on his obviously ancient mind.

Jack would've smiled if this wasn't so serious. When did his little girl grow up? She was supposed to be playing with dolls and dress-up, not boys and make-up.

Shit.

The crunch was, she was still his baby and he wanted her to be happy. But if he said the wrong thing, she'd think he was being mean. Which he absolutely wasn't, at least not deliberately. And how long did he have to ride this roller coaster anyway?

He gave in to the inevitable. "Where are you and *Ned* going?"

Her laughter bubbled through the airwaves, warming his heart. "The Soda Shoppe I think, and it's *Ted*, Daddy, as you very well know." She paused, and then in a voice soft as down she blanketed his heart with tenderness, "I know this is hard for you. I promise not to be late. Love you, Dad."

"Me too," he answered, swallowing a lump the size of Manhattan Island, and reluctantly let her go.

Now what?

Jack had spent so many years picking Tina up and dropping her off, whether it be dance class, skating, or soccer, that now he wasn't quite sure what to do with himself. Her mother had walked out on both of them when Tina was still a baby and it had been the two of them ever since. Sixteen, tumultuous, joyous years that he would never, ever regret.

Restless, Jack pushed back his chair, grabbed his hat from the peg, swung open the door, and swore. Instead of his usual diligent group of officers hard at work at their desks, they were all gathered in a tight knot around the front counter.

And his new secretary.

Jack still couldn't believe he'd let Angie talk him into hiring her while she went on vacation. Angie Sorenson hadn't taken a holiday since the day he'd taken office, so why she decided she needed to now, just when Tidal Falls seemed to be experiencing a crime spree, he didn't know. And the replacement she'd picked out... needless to say, he'd be happy when his life got back to normal.

He cleared his throat. Loudly. All chatter stopped and the group turned as one.

Mike Randolph was the first to answer. "Sorry boss, she needed help with the file cabinet." He blushed and moved his lanky butt back to his desk.

Norm Walters just shrugged his behemoth shoulders and strolled away smiling after handing the troublemaker his card.

Last to leave was Sid the squid, named for all the bullshit that spewed out of his mouth. He ignored Jack to lean over the counter and stage whisper the latest too-good-not-to-pass-on gossip. "Seriously, Miss, you should have seen him. The sheriff there wrestled that cougar to the ground all by hisself. The Hendersons say it was the craziest thing they ever seen."

Jack grimaced. That wasn't quite the way it happened. He'd been lucky to get a tranq into the mountain lion just as it jumped him. Thankfully the dart was fast-acting and took effect immediately, with the big cat literally falling from the sky to land at his feet.

"Okay, Squid, quit filling her ears with your blarney. Aren't you supposed to be doing a tour of the highway about now?"

Sid grumbled and rubbed at his whiskered chin, before doffing his hat like a gentleman courting his lady. Then he shoved it on over his batwing ears and stomped out the door.

Left with no more barriers, Jack forced himself to politely acknowledge the replacement. Now that her admirers had left she pretended to look busy straightening files and posting sticky notes to every available surface she could find. Curiosity almost had him leaning over the counter to see what she'd written, but just then she picked up a stapler and he decided a little distance might be wise.

He'd have to have a talk with her about her dress code. This wasn't the beauty section in a fancy department store. How did she plan to type with those inch long flamingo pink nails? And maybe she thought placing her honey-red hair up in a bun was professional, but all it did was bring about thoughts of the naughty secretary. It was... distracting.

Her white shirt, while business-like, highlighted perky breasts and creamy skin. His gaze followed the trail from the two undone buttons to her slender throat, stubborn chin with a hint of a cleft, pursed pink lips, and finally, golden brown eyes that knew just what they did to a man.

Angie was going to owe him big for this.

Katy was in trouble the moment Ty put his arms around her. Long buried feelings bubbled to the surface and threatened to run over, making an impossible situation that much worse. She wanted to believe what was happening between them was a residual of their past, but in her heart she was afraid it was more.

They had to sit down and have that talk soon. She needed to know he forgave her for leaving the way she did, even though if he cared he could have followed her, or at least called. And she needed to tell him what happened after she left.

"I can walk," she said, even as her hands tightened their grip around his shoulders. Helpless to stop, her fingers found and teased the fine curls at the base of his neck.

His breathing increased, and his arms squeezed a warning. "Quit that, or I'm not going to be responsible for what comes next."

Undaunted and enjoying her momentary sense of power, Katy set her lips against Ty's carotid artery, and licked. The vein against her mouth jumped in reaction. A second later they were through the door and the tables had turned. He dropped her to her feet, slammed the door shut, and pinned her to its wooden frame like a prize butterfly.

His blue eyes glinted at her from out of the shadows, the heat in their mesmerizing depths unmistakable. His hands were manacles that held her wrists to the wood. A muscled thigh pressed between her legs, holding her on her toes. A feral smile twisted his lips.

"If you play with fire," he murmured. "Expect to get burned." His mouth moved to within a hairsbreadth of hers. "My turn," he said huskily, before changing her world forever.

Her fingers curled at the first feather-light touch of his quicksilver lips. They were everywhere at once, setting off fiery little explosions in their wake. He roved at will, from the lobe of her ear and along the line of her jaw, to the tip of her nose and each eyelid in turn. No spot left untouched, except that which craved him the most. Her mouth.

His leg set up a forward and back motion, rocking her core until she wanted to scream in frustration.

"Ty," she moaned, thrashing against the door. Desperate now to break free so she could touch him and have his hands on her body. "Ty, kiss me."

She felt his smile against her cheek. "Now that's against the rules." But he did lower their arms so he could bring her hand to his lips. Nudging gently, he opened her fingers one by one, and sucked them into his mouth, keeping rhythm with his leg.

It was too much. It wasn't near enough.

Katy yanked her hands free and grabbed his head, pulling it down to her eager lips. "Didn't you teach me rules are meant to be broken?"

She was awash in sensation. Their past and what was happening now, in this moment, swirled inside her chest like a tidal pool, threatening to drag her under. His oh-so-talented tongue danced with hers to a tune only the two of them could hear. The taste was better than the richest chocolate bar, and just as decadent.

His hands roved over her hips and waist and moved much too slowly toward her aching breasts. Katy's heart stopped, waiting for the first touch. And when it happened; it was like a jolt from a defibrillator, life-changing. Every nerve strained closer, tuned to his every move. So focused, that she gave a shriek of surprise when he suddenly bent forward and lifted her over his shoulder. Then he turned, hand splayed across her butt, and strode down the hall.

A draft of cool air across her back where her shirt had lifted gave Katy a clue to where he was taking her; the hot tub.

"Aren't you a little old for this Neanderthal stuff?" she asked, hands braced on his back, just before he pitched her into the water.

Katy came up sputtering, her hair hanging in bedraggled clumps across her face. She brushed them back impatiently and glared at her tormentor.

"What the hell was that for?"

Contrary to the smirk she expected to see on his face, Ty stood at the edge of the pool and stared down at her with profound regret. "You tempt me more than any woman I've ever known, but I've realized I have a little pride after all.

"I'm not here to play second fiddle while your fiancé is out of town." He cursed and turned away, "I'm going for a shower. There are towels on the shelf. You can clean up and rest in the first room down the hall. I'll see you later."

He strode away without a backward glance, which Katy was grateful for because there was no way to hide the tears streaming down her cheeks.

CHAPTER FIFTEEN

Katy didn't expect to get any rest after the events of the afternoon, so she was surprised to awaken to a dim room. The muted lighting outside the window and her empty tummy told her it had to be near dinnertime. She lay for a moment longer to get her bearings, then threw back the light cover on the bed. Cool air brushed against skin and reminded her of the cataclysmic events of the day.

Ty had kissed her like there was no tomorrow. As if they were the only two people on earth. But they weren't. And she had a commitment to Jeff. He'd been right to stop when he had, not that she'd appreciated his method at the time. Whether or not they ever had a second chance together, Katy hated what she knew she had to do, but there was no choice. She couldn't go through with marrying Jeff feeling the way she did for Ty.

Jeff would be hurt. He genuinely cared about her. But she couldn't see herself building a life with him now, or having children together. Her fingers went to her flat tummy. A vision of a tow-headed boy with her eyes made her swallow convulsively.

Ouch. That hurts.

Katy's hand went to her sore throat and the earlier part of the afternoon crept through her mind like an unwanted intruder. She shivered and reached for the damp clothes she'd left draped across the foot of the bed. They were gone. Her gaze went to the closed door, Ty must have checked on her after she fell asleep.

Warmth flowed into her chest, displacing the ugly specter of her assailant, though her heart still wept for poor Doc Johnson.

She noticed a plaid robe folded on a sturdy looking Victorian wooden rocking chair and wrapped herself in its voluminous folds. The soft cotton retained the spicy pine laden scent of its owner. Katy buried her nose in the collar and breathed in the peaceful aroma. A soft sigh escaped. It was crazy how much had changed in the space of a couple of too-short days.

Maybe Ty was right and she was simply operating on a sensory overload. Everything had happened too fast for her to make an informed decision, no matter what her heart said.

She wandered over to the rapidly darkening window and gazed out at the shadows draping themselves over the leafless branches. The wind twisted and yanked in a fierce tug-a-war, determined to free the captive trees. She leaned her forehead against the cool glass and tried to ignore the foreboding shiver coursing up her spine. Kyle was the one who believed in listening to warning whispers. She'd always scoffed at his dire forecasts.

So why hadn't she believed him when he'd alerted her to the fact that their family was imploding? Instead, she'd closed her eyes and ears to the situation until it was too late. And when Katy tried talking to Ty about having to leave with her mom, he'd chosen to believe she was just looking for a way to move on. Harsh, vindictive words were said on both sides and that was the last time she saw him. Until now.

With the benefit of hindsight, Katy could see they'd both been too young for the intensity of their relationship. It was doomed to failure, though it was the best two years of her life.

The last thought strengthened her spine. Now that she was back and realized what they'd shared together was stronger than a teenage romance, it made her determined to sort out their differences and see if they stood a second chance. Life was too short to waste on misunderstandings. She wanted the dream of a life shared with her best friend, and the love of her life, Ty Garrett.

Now she just had to convince him.

Jack's gaze finally lifted from his fascination of a set of pearly white teeth worrying a lush pink bottom lip to find anxious brown eyes trained on him. They made him restless, those eyes.

"Well, Miss…" he hesitated, suddenly aware that he didn't even know her name yet.

"Thomas, Laurel Thomas," she said in a lyrical voice that threatened to crack at the seams. Her nails tapped out a nervous tune on the arms of her chair.

Jack hoped he wasn't going to have to babysit a scared rabbit while Angie was away. He didn't ask for much at the office except for efficiency. There was nothing more annoying than searching for a file that was misplaced due to negligence. This—woman— wasn't exactly inspiring much confidence within him of her abilities.

"Well, Miss Thomas, I imagine Angie apprised you of your duties?" She nodded, her topknot slipping a little to the starboard. "Great. So the next time the phone is ringing off the hook, do you suppose you could let me know, please?"

Maybe he was coming off a bit harsh, but damn it, he didn't have time to molly-coddle some beautiful young temptress.

Those nails of hers flexed and then dug gouges into the vinyl and Jack's back broke out in a cold sweat. Just what he didn't need right now, an unwanted attraction. His relationship with Annie Campbell was drawing to an end, and even though they hadn't dated for long, he was going to miss her. He was better off alone, especially now when he needed to be vigilant between everything that was happening in his town, and his daughter's budding independence.

Laurel pulled her ever-dwindling supply of post-it notes closer, bent over the pad to write a quick message, and passed the little yellow square to Jack.

He avoided the sticky edges and glanced down. What he saw written in almost childish cursive brought a wry smile to his lips.

The phones are ringing off the hook.
Sir.

So she was a wise guy. He could deal with that much easier than some vulnerable, down on her luck young woman looking for a man to solve her problems for her. He'd been down that road, it was a dead end.

Jack turned the square over, held out his hand and quirked an eyebrow at her until she gave up her weapon of choice, a pen with pink hearts all over the barrel.

Good thing or you wouldn't be needed, Miss Thomas.

He passed the note over, watched her cute little smirk turn upside down, and hid his own grin. "Now that we've gotten the pleasantries over with, I'm stepping out for dinner. If any calls come in, *forward them immediately.*" Jack placed extra emphasis on the last three words and waited. When nothing was forthcoming, he placed his hat on his head and turned for the door, whistling his satisfaction with getting his point across.

"Sir."

Jack slowed and glanced over his shoulder. "Yes, Miss Thomas?"

Her eyes sparkled as she held out her pink-tipped fingers, "Can I have my pen back, please?"

Jack reached into his shirt pocket and sure enough, he withdrew a girly pen covered in hearts.

Score: one-nothing for the new kid on the block.

He handed the evidence over, ignored her knowing smirk, and escaped with his dignity while he still could. It was his own fault, Angie asked him to sit in on the interviews and he'd begged off. Jack hated cross-examining prospective employees. Hearing how much each person needed the job, and then having to say no to him or her was just too damn hard.

The wind had picked up and threatened to steal his hat when he stepped out the door. Jack covered his mouth and nose with his arm and held tight to his hat while leaves danced down the street amid mini twirling tornadoes of dust and debris.

"Crazy west coast weather," he muttered, hurrying to his car parked on the far side of the lot. He'd just pulled his keys out when he thought he heard a voice calling his name over the windstorm. Brow furrowing, he turned, and sure enough, the figure of a man wearing camo pants and a heavy looking military jacket with a multitude of zippered pockets strode across the pavement towards him. Still twitchy from the afternoon's events, Jack's hand rested lightly on his weapon.

The stranger paid attention and slowed his step. "Hey man, don't shoot. I'd hate to think I travelled halfway around the world to get shot at home."

Something about the guy's cocky grin struck a familiar note. Jack catalogued his features one-by-one, short wheat colored hair, tired green eyes that saw too much, and a bristly jaw in need of a razor. Wide shoulders and a lean body spoke of a physically fit athlete, or… a soldier. Suddenly all the i's dotted and t's crossed.

"Well holy shit, look what the cat dragged in. Kyle Fowler. How the hell are you?" Jack reached out and pumped his old friend's hand. "It's been awhile. You look like crap, man. Don't they feed you in the army?" He grinned and slapped a meaty bicep.

"If you hadn't chickened out at the last minute, you'd know what real food is, my friend." Kyle joked. Army food was notorious for its blandness; meant to fill you up, not win any MasterChef contests.

Jack remembered how much he'd wanted to run away and join the circus that was the army with Kyle. The only thing that stopped him was his then six-year-old daughter. He couldn't walk away and leave her with the woman who'd given birth to her. He refused to call her a mother. She'd never even tried to be one to the little girl who adored her.

"My loss." He shrugged off the old regrets and smiled. "Listen, I was just about to go for dinner. Why don't you come with me and we can catch up? I want to hear what I missed."

Kyle hesitated and glanced over his shoulder, squinting past the surges of wind. "I'm actually trying to catch up to my sister. Have you seen her yet? She's supposed to be overseeing the restoration of the theatre for the wedding." His eyes were worried when they came back to Jack's face.

It would be better for Katy if Jack could defuse the bomb before it exploded when Kyle heard of his sister's attempted abduction. "Yeah, I've seen her. She's busy preparing for the big day. There was a situation today…" Kyle jerked and Jack held up a pacifying hand. "She's okay. Come for dinner and I'll tell you all about it."

Jack hoped he was doing the right thing by keeping the siblings apart for a while longer, but the look on

Ty's face this afternoon had told him more than words ever could. His brother was still crazy in love with that girl. He deserved a chance to make things right between them.

He decided to entertain Katy's brother for a couple of hours and then they could go over to Ty's. He still had to take their statements on the murder anyway. "Let's go, I'll show you what real food tastes like."

CHAPTER SIXTEEN

Ty scowled at the darkening skies and wind-whipped trees outside his living room window. He should probably go and check on Katy's clothes in the dryer, but remained slouched in his favorite leather chair, a near empty glass of scotch on the rocks resting loosely in his hand. She would be waking up soon and then they would have to decide on a course of action until her assailant was captured.

Every time he thought about her lying unconscious in that dusty alley like a broken doll his heart stopped. Literally.

All he could remember was screaming, *"No!"* He'd raced to her side and fell to his knees beside Grace. Her cheeks stained with tears, she gently folded Katy into his shaking arms. Then he'd prayed like he'd never prayed in his life. The sheer relief when she moaned and snuggled up into his chest would stay with him for the rest of his existence. Ty had wished everyone away in that moment, wanting, needing, to declare his everlasting love for the woman he held.

That feeling was reinforced when Doc Johnson was shot and bled out between his fingers shortly after, proving how vulnerable and precious the human body truly is and how swiftly it all could come to an end. He hoped Jack had made some headway on the case, because if Ty got his hands on the son-of-a-bitch first there wouldn't be enough left to arrest.

He finished his drink and set the glass down on an end table with careful precision instead of giving into the urge and hurling it across the room to relieve his stress like he wanted to do. He rose, closed the blinds blocking out the now stormy black skies, and made his way to the laundry room. He haphazardly folded her cotton underthings and tried to ignore his rising hunger for her silky skin.

A raging beast rose in his heart when he found the tear in the neckline of her shirt. What if Grace and her employee hadn't stepped into the alley just then? What if that animal had managed to drag Katy away? He slammed a fist down on top of the dryer, denting the machine. It didn't bear thinking about.

He gathered up the rest of her clothes and strode through the house to her room, halting at the closed door. Should he knock? Leave the clothes on her bed where he found them? It had been hard enough to walk away from her sleeping form the last time, he didn't trust himself now. But before their relationship could stand a chance, *if* it stood a chance, she had to end her engagement to the tycoon.

Decision made, he stooped over to place the items on the floor just as the door swung open and a set of pink tipped toes greeted him. His gaze travelled up shapely bare calves and ended regretfully on the tail of his plaid robe. Ty rose, clothes in hand, and stared down at his biggest temptation. Her hair was mussed from the pillow, her cheeks too pale, and her throat mottled with blue-black bruises.

Fuck.

"Hi," she whispered, her voice husky, either from her nap or that asshole's hands. His anger must have transmitted to her, because she nervously tightened the belt of the robe and drew the collar up to her chin.

"Don't," he said. "It wasn't your fault, so don't try to hide away from me." Ty stretched out a finger to run it gently down her cheek, hating her instinctive flinch. He wanted to tell her everything would be okay, that nothing would ever harm her like that again, but it was a promise he couldn't give.

Ty gave her some space by moving past to set her stuff down on the white wicker dresser. This was one of his favorite rooms in the house. Done with a feel for the sea, the walls were painted in a soothing shade of navy with white accents picked up by the wicker furniture. There was a giant unframed print on the side wall depicting a balcony with open windows, drifting white sheers, and an endless expanse of ocean beyond.

"I hope the room was all right," he said, not sure what to do with his hands now they were empty.

She nodded and moved to straighten the covers on the bed. The sway of her hips beneath his robe almost unmanned him. Hypnotized by her hands as they plumped up the pillow and traced the hem of the sheet with delicate fingers, Ty swallowed hard and swore under his breath.

"Pardon me?" She turned and caught him staring. His arousal was hard to miss, and her eyes on him only made it worse.

"I asked if you're hungry, it's almost dinner time." As soon as the words left his mouth he knew it was the wrong thing to say. Impossible not to think of the last time she'd been in this house for a meal and ended up as his dessert.

Invisible strings drew him across the room until he stood in her space, close enough to notice her agitated breathing and smell the musky scent of her desire.

"Ty..." she pleaded, her hands raised to push him away, or pull him closer, he wasn't sure. And the moment she made contact it didn't matter anymore. He gave in. Gave up.

"It's too late," he murmured as his arms drew her in. "I can't deny what's happening between us any longer. I need you. And you need me." His lips hovered ever closer, drawn to the heaven he knew awaited him within her embrace.

"God Katy, please say yes."

Trapped in the sensual web of Ty's gaze, Katy hardly knew her own name, much less the rights or wrongs of what they were about to do. And they *were* going to do it this time, she could see his surrender in his eyes, feel it in the arms wrapped around her as if he'd never let go. She hoped he wouldn't. There was nowhere else she wanted to be.

She reveled in the texture of his bare chest where he'd crushed her hands between their bodies. The firmness of muscle, the warmth of skin, the heart pounding beneath his breast. All for her.

Katy's head fell back and her lips opened of their own volition. His eyes flared with triumph but she didn't mind. They were both winners in this battle.

"I can't say no," she breathed out the words that set forth a fire in both their bodies. Ty groaned his relief and sighed her name, sending shivers of response over Katy's flesh. The moment their mouths touched, she knew she was home.

He was her haven.

Her arms slipped around his neck, tugging him closer. His wicked tongue drove her wild with a need only Ty could quench.

She whimpered when he took a step backwards, but he only wanted access to the knot of her belt. As his usually dexterous fingers fought the tie, he met her teary eyes with a grave look of his own.

"Okay?" he asked, holding the edges of the loosened cloth together.

If she hadn't loved him heart and soul before, Katy would have fallen hard now. She nodded, too overcome for words, and grasped his hands to help with her unveiling. She had an anxious moment when the robe slid from her shoulders. Her body was not the one he would remember. Young and slim had been taken over by fullness and maturity. What if she didn't physically please him anymore? Embarrassed, she reached for the fallen robe, but Ty's hands stopped her movement.

"Don't," he whispered, his voice gruff. "I just want to look at you."

Katy straightened and forced herself to look him in the eye. The heat of his gaze did much to warm her heart, this man who knew her so well, yet not at all.

"You're so fricken beautiful." He tugged her forward and kissed her so reverently tears sprang up and rolled down her cheeks. He brushed them aside with his thumbs and then kissed her eyelids closed before sliding back to her mouth, as though he couldn't get enough.

Katy licked his lips and tasted her tears, smiling a little at the soft sound of want that rumbled up from his chest. His mouth turned firm, demanding, and she opened more, wanting all that heat for herself. He tasted of scotch and lust, an irresistible combination. Her hands enjoyed the feel of tensile strength in the muscles bunching beneath her fingertips. His biceps were those of a man not afraid of manual labor.

They made her hot.

Achy.

Ty's hands were everywhere at once. He swept through her hair, tugging her head back so his mouth could have better access. He massaged her back, making her moan in delight. His fingers gripped her bum and lifted her closer to his hardness, his jeans a rough abrasion that turned her wild. He nipped her bottom lip and she gasped before returning the favor.

He growled, and raising her completely off the floor, turned and dropped her backward with a bounce onto the bed. His eyes flared hotter than a Texas sky.

Katy yelped, then stilled as his hands went to the snap on his jeans. One pop and a zip and her breathing all but stopped. He must have been in a hurry after his shower, he forgot to put on any shorts. She giggled nervously.

Ty's hands stilled in the process of pushing his pants off his hips. He eyed her curiously, an upward curve of the lips lightening the almost unbearable expectation in the room.

"Just so you know, a guy doesn't expect laughter when he drops his drawers." He let his fall to the floor and stepped out of them. "It's hard on our pride."

Well, something was certainly hard, but Katy didn't think pride had much to do with it. "You talking, or performing?" She leaned back on her arms throwing her breasts into prominence. Two could play that game.

"Oh, I'm performing, lady. Just you wait and see." He threw a string of those glow-in-the-dark condoms he'd pulled out of his pocket onto the bed and then followed them down, pretending to crush her under his body, and Katy shrieked in mock fright. In reality his hands stopped his fall, but it was enough to sober them up in a hurry when soft sleek skin met hard firm muscle in an explosion of sensation.

The hair on Ty's chest rubbed the nipples on Katy's breasts and her eyes slid closed in reaction to the touch. His legs, one on the outside, and the other between hers, were warm and strong leaving her feeling safe and secure within his hold. Her tongue slipped out to wet suddenly dry lips. He dipped his head and caught up the moisture before dropping to her breast and laving the nipple. The catlike feel of his tongue sent ripples of shock like a current straight to her core. Katy's back arched in helpless reflex, sighing when Ty settled more fully into the apex of her thighs. The relief was only temporary. An aching emptiness had her shifting under him as she tried to find a way to ease the throbbing.

"Shh, baby, I've got you." Ty rumbled. His hand moved down her side and over her tummy until he rubbed against her center. Katy's mouth opened in a soundless cry of ecstasy. Her whole body straightened out like a board for endless seconds before falling back to earth and the softness of the mattress.

It took her a few moments to open her eyes to Ty's satisfied smile.

"Wow," she murmured, a little embarrassed at how fast she'd climaxed.

"That was amazing," Ty said, his gaze warming her cheeks.

"I'm sorry," she said, uncomfortably aware of his arousal nestled against her belly.

"Why? I'm not." He grasped her hand and brought it to his lips before handing her a condom. Then he lowered her fingers to his swollen cock, which jumped and lengthened even more at the contact. "Feel that? That's what you do to me. Every. Single. Time."

Fascinated with the strangled nuance of his voice, Katy tested her power by stroking the silken club beneath her fingertips as she rolled the latex from top to bottom. The engorged head wept in response. Ty groaned and the next thing she knew he moved and encased himself deep within her body.

Time stopped.

Staring into his beloved face, it was almost like they'd never been apart. Katy reached up and brushed his damp hair off his brow and then turned her head and kissed the arm holding his weight above her.

"I need you," she whispered, meeting his tender gaze. Then he began to move, and the world faded away.

Ty lay on his side watching the woman he adored more than his life. Her lashes were half moon crescents upon her creamy cheeks. Her hands, folded together as though in prayer, rested under her sleeping face like an angel and her body lay sideways, taking up most of the bed. He didn't care, it was a miracle that she was here at all. One he'd prayed often for.

He wondered if she remembered how they used to cruise the neighborhoods dreaming of the perfect home to raise their family. When they came across this house in Cedar Grove, Katy had fallen in love with it at first sight. They'd spent hours down the lane watching the family that lived here at the time. Compared to her house, this was nothing more than a bungalow, but she didn't care. She told him love made a house a home and the rest didn't matter.

He'd begun saving right then and there. If the house ever came up for sale he wanted to be ready. It wasn't easy, his job as an errand boy at a mechanics shop hadn't paid much. Ty was just grateful his boss let him work on his old beater after hours to keep it running. The car might not have looked like much, but it gave him and Katy a place to be together and that was the important thing. That Ford had witnessed his transition from a boy to a man. It was also the place he gave his heart to the woman beside him now.

As though she could feel his gaze, Katy's sleepy lids opened with a warm glow of contentment. Then, just as he moved forward to kiss her, a shadow fell over her face.

"Ty, there's something you need to know." The words seemed to stick in her throat and his stomach tumbled.

"Ookay, as long as you're not going to say you're dying or something," he warned, only half joking.

The words when they came, fell with all the subtleness of a bomb.

"I was pregnant when I left Tidal Falls. The baby was yours."

CHAPTER SEVENTEEN

Kyle sat in the passenger seat of the sheriff's sporty Ford Mustang GT and grinned when Jack grabbed second and burned a little rubber leaving the station. Kyle appreciated the rumble of power coming from the Ford's dual exhaust pipes as those eight cylinders did their job and set him back in his seat.

Kids and their toys, guess you are never too old to enjoy the need for speed.

That was his excuse every time he went up in the belly of a Hurricane 'copter and felt his heart soar with the thrill of the ride. Then there were the endless moments of pure adrenaline while plummeting toward earth with only a mushroom cloud of nylon stopping him from becoming an ink splat on God's canvas.

Kyle was a little surprised that this was Jack's choice of vehicle though. He'd always pictured him as a four door sedan type of guy. Mind you, becoming a father at the age of seventeen couldn't have been an easy thing to do. Put a quick end to Jack's football scholarship. Put an end to a lot of things. Suddenly Ty's superhero brother became as human as the rest of them.

"So how's army life treating ya?" Jack glanced over as he shifted down for one of the two traffic lights Tidal Falls sported. "You stuck with it a lot longer than I figured you would."

He wasn't the only one.

"It's good. I enjoy the camaraderie, and the babes aren't bad either." That was a side benefit of wearing those badges, women love a man in uniform. And if that seemed a bit jaded, Kyle figured after ten years in the forces he'd earned the right. Every relationship he'd ever had went south the moment he deployed. In his experience, with the exception of his mother and sister, women couldn't be trusted.

The light turned green and Jack coasted through to the other side, pulling into the only spot open in front of the stucco and brick façade of Grits and Grace. The rapidly darkening evening provided a backdrop for the action going on behind the plate glass windows. Customers filled the booths, some eating and some looking at menus, while the servers raced up and down the aisles with food and drink piled high on trays that looked too large for their arms to handle.

Jack shut off the engine and pulled his keys. "You ready to eat?" he asked as he pushed open the door and climbed out.

Kyle nodded, but hoped they didn't have to wait long for a table. The need to see Katy was growing by the moment. He opened his door and started to step out when he noticed the courtesy light provided the lit figure of a mustang running on the pavement at his feet. He turned and lifted his brow at Jack, impressed even though he wouldn't openly admit it. "Special effects, much?"

Jack just grinned and closed his door. Then his gaze landed on some yellow tape running across the entry to the alley beside the café and his expression sobered. Curious, Kyle joined him on the walk and nodded toward the obvious crime scene.

"Trouble in paradise, Sheriff?"

"Yeah, something like that. C'mon, let's get inside before there are no tables to be had." He strode to the diner's glass door and yanked it open.

Kyle hesitated as that uneasiness brushed up against his spine again, then shrugged and followed him inside.

Ty threw himself back on his pillow and stared at the ceiling, the words reverberating in his head, *"He was yours. He was yours. He was..."* mine.

A baby.

He'd had a little boy and never even known.

Fuck.

He started to hyperventilate. His body vibrated with the need to move.

Now.

Ty jumped from the bed as though it was full of snakes and headed down the dark hallway, his bare ass flapping in the wind. He didn't care. He just needed some air before he did something he might regret. Using more force than he'd intended, the patio door slammed open, and a few long strides later he gasped as his body hit the cool water in the pool. The liquid churned as he power-stroked through a few fast laps before the worst of the shock eased off and his stroke evened out.

He didn't know how long he stayed there, but when he finally came to a stop, his arms resting on the flagstones surrounding the pool and his chest heaving, Katy was there. Waiting.

She crouched in front of him. Silent tears rolled unheeded down her cheeks. Lightning flickered across the sky behind her lowered head.

"I'm sorry, Ty. I should have told you."

He ignored the underlying need to comfort her and ease her pain. Who was going to help the soul-stealing ache he was feeling? The one person in the world that he'd always trusted more than any other had managed to pull the wool over his eyes for the very last time.

He was done. They were done.

"Where is he? With your darling parents?" His laugh turned bitter. "They never did think I was good enough for their precious baby girl, did they."

Katy sniffled and held out a shaking hand to touch him. He recoiled, not at all sure what might happen if she did.

"I'm not going to ask again." Each word was a whip meant to flail her alive. To make her hurt even an eighth of what he was going through right now. "Where. Is. My. Son?"

Her fingers scrubbed at colorless cheeks before she rose and turned away from him.

"Katy?"

"I don't know where he is," she whispered. "I don't even know if he's alive." Her back hunched as though to receive a blow. "I gave him up when he was a newborn." Her shoulders trembled. "I gave our son away."

Ty shook his head, and droplets of water flew in all directions. He was pretty sure she just said she gave their son away. Like a piece of furniture. But that couldn't be true. Could it?

He heaved himself out of the pool, grabbed a towel from a nearby cupboard to wrap around his hips, and strode to her side to demand an answer. Ty paused when he saw how distraught she'd become. He sighed. It couldn't be easy for her either, having to confront the past like this.

He turned her into his chest and wrapped his arms around her shivering body. They'd have to head inside soon or she'd catch her death of cold. His chin rested on top her head and they slowly rocked from side to side.

"Shh, it's going to be okay." Then after another moment when she showed no sign of easing up, "Quit crying now, you're soaking me."

That got a half-fast laugh out of her. A few more hiccupping sobs and she pulled herself together. She swiped her nose, then lifted her head and bravely met his eyes.

"I'm sorry, Ty. More sorry than you can ever imagine. I wanted to tell you as soon as I knew I was pregnant, but my mom was a mess with my dad leaving her and everything. It just wasn't the right time. And then afterward... afterward there wasn't much left to say."

She gave a little self-depreciating shrug. "It was easier to push it under the carpet and try to forget about it, you know?" Her eyes beseeched him to believe her. "It's not an excuse, and I'm really, really sorry, but that's what happened."

Ty's feelings were ping ponging around in his chest like this was a championship match. Anger, sorrow, sympathy, and disappointment fought for supremacy. In the end sympathy won the battle. Her slouched shoulders and dull eyes made it clear the decision had weighed heavy on her these past years. He wasn't sure if they could get past her betrayal. It hurt too much right now to contemplate, so he kept to the basics.

"Why did you give him up?" He loosened his hold and stepped back a couple paces, needing some space between them right now. "I don't understand. It couldn't have been a money issue, your family is loaded. So, what then? How could you give up your own flesh and blood?"

He lifted his hand to rub tiredly at the base of his neck, absently noting a few random drops of rain hitting the flagstones. The wind was chilly and they needed to get inside, but all he could think about was his child in someone else's arms. Jesus, he'd be almost ten by now. So many wasted years. The anger made a return trip.

Katy held out her hands, pleading, and he didn't think he'd ever seen a sorrier sight. She'd slipped on his robe to come looking for him. It hung unevenly on her slight frame, one side dragging the ground while the other flipped around her ankles in the wind. Her hair could have happily accommodated an entire family of sparrows, and her face was blotchy from too many tears. None of it mattered; his heart still ached with love and tenderness, even though she'd hid something so vital it damn near crippled him to think about it.

"I don't know if I can properly explain." Her voice was small and her hands fell to worrying the ends of the belt.

"When my father betrayed my mother it changed our lives. I was whisked away without any choice to California. Dad and Kyle were gone. *You* were gone." She gazed at him with a lost look. "Mom was a mess. She counted on me for everything and I couldn't let her down. She needed me, Ty."

He shook his head. "I needed you."

"I had to make a choice. I couldn't walk away from her like that, I just couldn't."

Katy's words rang with the desperation she must have felt suddenly getting cast in the role of provider, at least emotionally, for her mom. Ty tried to understand, but at the same time he didn't get how she could have turned her back on them with such ease.

So he cut off whatever excuse she would've made, "Look, it's getting late, and I don't know about you, but this has been the day from hell for me." He turned away and strode for the French doors.

"Let's shelve this discussion for the evening and get some sleep. We can talk again in the morning, agreed?" He moved aside to let her pass and tried not to think about how few clothes stood between them.

He shivered from the warmth inside the house and realized just how chilled he'd become from standing around in almost nothing. Ty glanced at Katy and cleared his throat. "I'm, ah… going to take a quick shower. Do you want to check what's in the refrigerator while I'm gone?"

She gave a hesitant nod, obviously as reluctant as he was to enter that den of iniquity. He walked away before he decided to prove her right.

Katy stared after Ty as he took off down the hall like a scalded cat. This wasn't easy for either of them, but at least she'd had the benefit of time to dull her pain. Not that it ever truly disappeared. Birthdays and holidays were the hardest. She'd find herself trolling the toy store sites to find the newest and coolest items, from superhero costumes to Transformer play sets. Sometimes going so far as to place them in the cart before she realized there was no need. Then the depression would hit and she'd have to dive back into her work at the hospital or drive herself crazy.

It was hard not to hate the doormat she'd been as a teenager. Whatever her parents asked of her, she'd done. Why couldn't she have been more like Kyle and stood up for what she wanted? Her life would have been so different if only she had. She and Ty would have learned of their upcoming baby together and celebrated its birth as proud parents should. They could have built their life in this home—the home they'd chosen together so long ago—married, had more children and been happy as a family.

Instead, they were separated at the seams by conniving parents, much as a seamstress destroys a half-sown sweater one stitch at a time until everything unravels around their feet.

She'd told Ty her mom was an emotional wreck after finding out about her father's infidelity, and that was true. What Katy hadn't mentioned was how her mother manipulated her into leaving Tidal Falls, and him, behind. How she cried about needing her daughter at her side after losing first her son to the army, and then her husband to a younger woman.

Looking back on those events, Katy could see how she'd been influenced by her mom's very real grief into giving up her own dreams. The only freedom Katy had in those first few years was her schooling, and even that came at the direction of her mom. She would have been happy to become a family physician like Doc Johnson—tears surfaced again as she pictured him as she'd seen him last—but her mother determined her career would be as a surgeon. And Katy had let her.

That was the worst of it, she had no one to blame but herself for the mess her life had become. But that was the old Katy. Her shoulders straightened and she tightened the belt on her robe. This Katy knew what she wanted.

She just needed to figure out how to get him.

CHAPTER EIGHTEEN

Ramsey decided to let the dust settle for a few days and took a trip down to California. He strolled along the busy boardwalk of the Santa Monica Pier in the afternoon air and kept an eye out for the boss, enjoying the rare treat of a foot long New York style hot dog, complete with fried onions and piled high with sauerkraut.

Shit was going to hit the fan when Ramsey confessed to the shooting. There'd been no real choice though. The old man had gotten a good look at him as he made his escape. Now he was going to need some protection, and the boss could arrange for that to happen.

Frustration at his near miss with that bitch ate at his insides. It was girls like her who had tormented him his entire life. Hoity-toity, snooty women who wouldn't give him the time of day. After this job that would change. They say money can't buy love, but it sure as hell could buy some sweet fucks, and that was good enough for him. He'd never be stupid enough to fall for the whole *love* spiel anyway.

He watched some guy win his girl a giant stuffed Panda at the shooting gallery. The chick squealed her pleasure with the gift, gave the guy a peck on the cheek, then spun away to show off the prize to her friends.

Typical. Women were the human's version of the Black Widow spider. They hung around long enough to bleed a guy dry, and then they destroyed him. Game over.

Ramsey checked his watch. Almost time. He always made certain he arrived in place long before a meeting. That way he could take his time, watch the crowd, and make sure he wasn't getting set up. In his experience it was better to play it safe, than end up dead.

He threw his wrapper in the overflowing garbage bin, kept to the shadows of the buildings, and made his way over to the Ferris wheel. The irritating noises of the crowd blended with the carnival music and amped up his edginess. Then he caught sight of the familiar blue ball cap and relaxed.

The boss had arrived.

"What are you doing here? I thought I told you to follow my orders and keep an eye on my daughter."

Ramsey's hand fisted by his side, and then he forced a smile. "Don't worry, I'll take care of your daughter.

Katy debated following Ty down the hall, then decided to give him a little time to process. Maybe afterward they could talk without ripping each other apart. There was something she did need to do though, call Jeff. No sense putting off the inevitable. She couldn't marry one man while loving another.

Curled up on the leather sofa Katy reached for the landline sitting on the table. She dialed the memorized number, and listening to the ringing tone, inhaled a deep breath. A quick glance over her shoulder proved the hall was still empty just as the phone was picked up on the other end.

"Hello?" His familiar voice in the quiet room startled her. Guilt flooded her chest. Even though Katy hadn't meant to, she'd betrayed this man who meant so much to her. The man she would have married in a few short weeks.

But he wasn't Ty.

"Who is this? Katy?"

Oh yeah, caller ID. He probably recognized the area code. "Yes, it's me. Hi, Jeff." She stared across the room at a giant watercolor of the Cascade Mountains at sunrise, stunning.

"Where are you calling from? This isn't the hotel's number." His voice turned warm, beckoning, "I miss you, babe."

The mountains took on a misty hue.

Katy put a hand to her chest, blinking to clear her vision.

This is so hard.

"I miss you too, but that's actually not why I'm calling." He started to say something, but she cut him off, needing to get it out before this conversation got any more difficult. "I have something I have to tell you." Her voice hitched, filled with pent-up emotion. "I'm sorry, Jeff, but I have to cancel the wedding. I can't marry you any more."

Silence greeted her announcement. Well, what did she expect? One minute he's a happily engaged man looking forward to his wedding night, and in the next he finds out the woman who was to say I do in front of one hundred and fifty of their closest family and friends, now says I don't.

"I'm sorry," she repeated, her voice nothing more than a subdued murmur. "Please believe I never meant to hurt you." Her fingers plucked nervously at a couple of loose threads in the robe. "I care for you. Just not in the way a woman should love the man she plans on spending the rest of her life with."

Jeff sighed, "Are you sure?"

And then he released the saddest chuckle she'd ever heard. "I knew it was too good to be true almost from the moment I laid eyes on you. What's a girl like you going to see in a guy like me anyway, right?"

"That's not true. A woman would be lucky to have a man like you in her life. Please, believe that." Katy let out a little sob that she muffled with her fisted hand. "I... I need to go now. Take care, Jeff. I hope you can see your way clear so that we can still be friends. I'd miss not having you in my life."

"I'm not going to deny I'm stunned. I thought we had a good thing going, but if you're not happy I'm glad you found out before this became a whole bunch more complicated. Good-bye, sweetheart. No hard feelings—they may be somewhat bruised, but I'll survive."

He hesitated a moment before adding, "You know where to find me if you have a change of heart." And then with a quiet click he was gone.

Katy cradled the phone against her breast for a moment before carefully setting it back in its resting place. The kitten jumped up and daintily stepped onto her lap. "Hi there, little one. How are you liking your new home?" She rubbed the top of her head and behind the ears, smiling past her tears at the cold engine sound of her purr.

So. That, was that. Two years of love and friendship gone in a couple of short long distance phone call minutes. It was the right thing to do, but that didn't make her feel any better. She fiddled with the ring she'd once worn with pride. Now it felt like an anchor pulling her down with the weight of her recent decisions.

Not the least of which was that maybe Doc Johnson would still be alive if only she hadn't stepped out that back door. It tightened the knot in her belly. Logically, she knew that it may have happened anyway. The man who'd grabbed her probably already had a police record. Maybe that's why he'd run when Jack stepped out to talk to him. It was her sheer misfortune to be in the wrong place at the right time.

She hoped Jack would arrest him soon and life could get back to normal, minus her wedding of course. At least she had time to figure things out before she was needed back in LA. Between the preparation time and the honeymoon, Katy had booked two months away from her job. The board was reluctant to agree at first, but since this was her only holiday in years, there wasn't a lot they could do.

Truthfully, she'd been unhappy with her life in California for some time now. Her mom was the main reason she'd stayed. Katy's mother was never the same after her husband's betrayal. The confident, successful woman had turned into one that had become needy and desperate.

Dissatisfied, Katy set the cat down, stood and skirted the edge of the couch to go to the kitchen and make a light dinner for her and Ty before he came back from his shower. Except, she was too late. He stood watching her from across the room. She gulped. His skin still carried a light sheen of moisture, causing it to glisten in interesting places on his bare chest—didn't the man own a shirt?

His abs—holy moly his abs—were well delineated, and pointed the way to his happy trail which in turn lead into the unbuttoned top of faded, form-fitting jeans that had her practically salivating. The man was sex on a stick and acted as if he didn't know, or care. His gaze, in contrast, was solemn under his towel brushed hair.

"You okay?" He edged a little closer. "I couldn't help but overhear your phone call. So you broke it off with the big shot, huh?"

Katy's lips quirked upward. Trust Ty to cut to the chase. "I did, yes. It wasn't easy, but after... you know, us, it wouldn't have been fair to continue on with the ceremony."

He nodded his head and stepped the last few feet until he was directly in front of her. Uncomfortable in her own skin, Katy stared at the masculine chest she'd lain beneath not long ago. It felt deceitful to turn away one man in hopes of attracting another.

There, she'd admitted it. She wanted Ty. Always had, and probably always would, no matter how this turned out between them.

Ty's index finger curled under her chin and gently lifted until Katy had no choice other than to meet his concerned, yet triumphant, gaze. "So, now you're single?" His tone coaxed an answer.

Much as she wanted to shout it from the rooftops, Katy also needed Ty's forgiveness. Something she feared might never happen. So for that reason she hesitated before replying, "Yes, but…"

"About damn time." His eyes glowed with warmth and happiness just before he swept her up in his arms and swung her around the room.

"Ty," she shrieked, laughing, her arms wrapped in a stranglehold around his neck. "Ty, put me down."

He did, but it was a slow, sweet slide down the length of his oh-so-fine body. And when her toes touched the ground, he kissed her. The whole world shrunk until there was no one else except one boy and one girl and a lifetime of loving one another. This was the reason Katy needed to come home. Not the theatre. Not the wedding. Just Ty.

His mouth seared as his tongue mated with hers in a ritual only lovers could share. The rising heat enhanced the fresh pine scent of his skin after the shower. His shoulders turned to malleable steel under her hands.

Excitement made Katy's breathing choppy and her heart race. There was little doubt where this was going to end. She loved how dominant Ty was in his desire. It made her feel delicate, yet strong. Precious, and yet his equal. They would be partners in this journey of the body and the soul.

She rubbed against him like a cat, her breasts aching for his touch, and he groaned. "I need you," he muttered. "Always and all ways."

Katy caught the distinction and her eyes flooded with tears of joy. Maybe they were going to be okay after all. He swept her up in his arms to carry her down the hall and her lips found his ear. She nuzzled and nipped until he nearly dropped her. He stopped to return the favor and goose bumps popped out on her arms and chest.

She squirmed and Ty lost his grip on the back of her legs. She slid to the floor, her head and shoulder blades thumping the wall behind her.

Ty lifted his head from her neck long enough to ask, "Shit, are you okay?"

Katy giggled, she couldn't help it. They were like their teenage counterparts, all legs and arms. She'd just opened her mouth to reassure him she was fine when the doorbell rang above their heads and startled them into silence.

Katy looked at him with raised brows and he shrugged, returning to her exposed neck. She shivered.

The doorbell rang again.

The consternation on his face would have been funny to see if not for the fact that she felt the same way.

Ty cursed, and after one last lingering kiss, he turned away and strode for the front door. Katy followed a few steps behind, curious as to who it could be. The door swung open and there stood a frowning Jack, still in uniform so this probably wasn't a social call.

Ty spoke first. "Anything yet?"

Jack swept his brother and then her a knowing look before answering, "No, but we'll get him. I need to take your statements. And there's someone here to see Katy."

Hearing her name, Katy stepped forward just as the sheriff moved out of the doorway. In his place stood her brother, Kyle.

"Kyle," she cried, and raced past Ty to jump into her twin's outstretched arms. "Oh, Kyle." And she burst into tears.

CHAPTER NINETEEN

Katy poured another cup of green tea for the men seated at Ty's scarred oak table. Grimness marked the men's faces and told of the frustration they all felt in regards to the missing attacker. Even though Jack had staff scouring every street, the man had managed to somehow disappear. She hoped for a break in the case soon, before someone else was injured.

She refilled the fruit and cheese tray and tried not to blush when Ty picked out a strawberry and slowly carried it to his mouth, his blue eyes shining with wicked delight. Katy frowned her mock disapproval and turned away in time to catch Kyle's speculative gaze.

Her brother seemed so much older, more mature, than the last time she'd seen him. His skin was tanned almost to teak by the hot Italian sun. There was a web of tiny creases near the outer edges of his eyes, and his mouth bore the look of someone who rarely found humor in life.

Katy nudged him with her shoulder as she sank onto the chair next to him, leaving Ty talking to Jack. "I can't believe you're here. It's been what, eighteen months or more?"

Kyle reached over and tweaked her nose. "Yeah, something like that. You could always come to Italy for a visit, you know."

She nodded and watched Ty mix a spoonful of sugar into his tea before sending an indecipherable glance toward her and Kyle. Then he turned and said something under his breath to his brother.

She didn't know what he was thinking, but if it had anything to do with her leaving town without him, forget it. At least not until after they'd had a chance to sort out their issues and determine whether their love could flourish given a second chance.

"I've been meaning to, it's just hard with the hospital. And you know how Mom can be." Katy smiled at her brother to prove she didn't really mind. When the split first happened, and Kyle left for the army, she admitted to feeling resentment at being the one left behind to pick up the pieces of her mother's life. But time and circumstance had dulled the bitterness.

Katy had tried to talk to him about their dad over the years, but to no avail. Kyle's agreement to attend the wedding was a giant step forward for all of them. It would be the first time he was in the same room with their father since the separation.

He grabbed a handful of plump red grapes and popped a couple in his mouth. "I'm surprised she's not here commandeering the whole thing."

"Kyle," Katy reprimanded. "Give her a chance. She's different now." The two of them had always butted heads. He'd been daddy's boy, while Katy was her mother's little princess. She'd never had the time for his rambunctious little boy's curiosity.

"I'll believe that when I see it. I'm only in this for you, no one else." He warned, chewing on another grape.

She blinked back sudden tears; fiercely glad he'd decided to come early, before he learned of the cancelled nuptials. Which reminded her, "Why *are* you here? The wedding wasn't for another month."

That got his undivided attention, along with Jack and Ty's.

Oops.

He frowned. "What the H E double L do you mean was?"

She turned to Ty, who nodded encouragement.

"You mind telling me what's going on around here? And don't think I didn't notice those bruises on your neck either." Kyle waved a hand at her bathrobe and Ty's bare chest. "Or... *that.*" He glared at Ty, who grinned back.

Katy scowled across the table. "Not helping here."

She turned to her brother. "I didn't know until I came back home and saw Ty again..." He held out his hand and she latched on like a newborn babe. "I couldn't marry Jeff. Not while I'm in love with another man."

Oh boy, she'd said it out loud, in front of God, and everybody.

Ty's fingers tightened, pulling her attention to his tender gaze. "Well, I could think of a better place for your declaration." He urged her up and around the table until she stood looking down into his beloved face.

"I love you too, more than I ever thought possible." He chuckled and dragged her onto his lap. "Trust you to do the unexpected."

Then he kissed her.

Katy reached out and grabbed the only thing solid in her world, Ty's broad shoulders. In the back of her mind she waited for the other shoe to drop. Everything was almost too perfect.

Her brother was here, her nearly disastrous wedding had been avoided, and Ty had forgiven her. She swore this time around, no one was going to stop them from being together.

Ty ignored the whooping and hollering behind him and concentrated on the woman in his arms. Her mouth held a hint of sweetness from the honey she'd used in her tea, and something that was uniquely Katy. If they ever went onto one of those dating game shows he'd seen on TV he had no fears about telling her from the other contestants, blindfolded or not. The soft, womanly weight on his lap induced illicit thoughts of untying that sash and laying her out like a banquet for their mutual satisfaction. Wonder what she'd say if he burned all her clothes and kept her in his robe for the next ten years or so. Now that sounded like his idea of nirvana.

"*Uh-hem.*" Her brother's overly loud clearing of his throat penetrated Ty's sensual haze. He lifted his head from its foray of her neck and smiled into glowing moss green eyes.

"To be continued," he murmured, and rubbed his raspy chin against her smooth as silk cheek, smiling as she shivered in reaction. His hands straightened the front of her robe before he reluctantly let her regain her feet.

"It seems your brother is worried about my intentions, probably with good cause."

Katy blushed a becoming shade of pink that contrasted wildly with his tartan robe. "Ty, don't tease," she said, avoiding eye contact by cleaning off the remnants of their snack from the table and carrying the dishes to the sink. "He just wants me to be happy, right, Kyle?"

"Well you have to admit this *is* kind of sudden." His words were innocuous enough, but his gaze warned Ty not to fuck with his sister.

"Actually, my *friend*, this has been ten years in the making. Remember?" Ty understood, and was even grateful that Katy had such a strong support network. But enough was enough; he was on their side. They weren't the ones left wondering what the hell happened when the woman he planned on spending the rest of his life with had suddenly up and disappeared. He'd thought Kyle was as much his friend as Katy was his lover and so felt twice the betrayal.

"Okay, let's break up the reunion and stick to business for now." Ever the levelheaded, Jack clapped his brother on the back before glancing at Katy as she froze in the middle of loading the dishwasher. "You guys ready to give your statements yet?"

"Now?" Ty scowled.

Katy hurried over, sank onto her knee in her seat, and reached out to grasp Ty's taut forearm on the table. "It's okay, really, I'd like to get it over with."

"What's going on? Is this about the crime scene tape, Jack?" Kyle demanded, his chair creaking as he leaned forward to see all their faces.

"Take it easy," Jack said. "As I mentioned earlier, your sister was involved in an incident this afternoon, and as you can see, she's a little shook up but otherwise fine."

"And where the hell were you, loverboy?" Kyle snarled at Ty.

Ty's muscles tensed, ready for the fight he could see about to happen. "You're right, I should have been there, and if I'd known she was in possible danger, you can bet your ass I would never have left her alone."

"Kyle, stop accusing him. And Ty, it's my own damn fault. If I had kept out of the way, none of this would have happened and Doc Johnson wouldn't be dead." Katy's emotional words left a heavy silence in their wake.

Ty turned his arm over beneath her fingers and grasped her hand. "You didn't know he was dangerous. Don't beat yourself up because some asshole was trigger happy." He met her teary gaze and said what was in his heart. "I wanted to die when I saw you laying in that alley. You can't imagine my relief when those gorgeous eyes of yours opened. I never want to go through that again."

"I'm glad you were there," she answered softly. "I kept hoping you were already gone so you couldn't get hurt. I was so scared though."

"Did he say what he was after?" Jack asked.

She slid a nervous glance at Ty and slipped free of his hold, burying her hand in her lap before quietly replying. "He said he was there for me."

What?

Everything within Ty tightened. So the son-of-a-bitch thought he could go around molesting women, did he? Wait until he caught the fucker, there were tools in his truck that would have that asshole singing soprano for the rest of his miserable life.

"Do you have any idea why he was looking for you?" Jack, again.

"What the hell, man?" Ty glared at his brother.

"It's okay, Ty. He's just doing his job." Katy glanced at her grim brother, then away. "I think he just wanted to scare me, sheriff. He was hiding from you. When I happened on the scene he used me for cover." She hesitated for a brief moment, her fingers lifting to bruised flesh, before adding, "He said he was coming back for me."

"Jack, we..."

"That asshole can..."

Kyle answered at the same time as he did, both men ready to leap into action and see some justice served.

"Calm down, you two." Jack waved them back into their seats. "Going off half-cocked isn't going to do anybody any good. We need to be smart about this. He knows we're looking for him so he's going to lay low for a while. Our job..." he eyed each man in turn. "*Our job is going to be to draw the sum-bitch out.*"

CHAPTER TWENTY

Katy pulled up to the theatre with her brother and put her car in park. The past couple days had been filled with wedding cancellations and numerous explanations. Most of the vendors had accepted with good grace, merely holding onto their hefty deposits. But the family and friends were another thing altogether. They were all like greedy vultures wanting to know what went wrong. She'd tried to reach her mom a couple of times with no success so she finally just left a message for her to call. And when she reached her dad he had sounded both sympathetic and somewhat relieved.

"Why do you sound happy with my decision, Dad?"

"Maybe I don't want you making the same mistakes I made." It was the first time he'd ever intimated there might be more to the breakdown of their marriage than his unfaithfulness.

"Do you think we treated Dad unfairly?" Katy looked over to see her brother staring out the window at the half-finished theatre. His crew-cut hair, as blond as her own, caught the evening rays of the sun and formed a nimbus around his head.

When he turned his moody gaze upon her, Katy cringed. "No." The single syllable carried a multitude of pain and anger. "How can you even say that? He destroyed our family."

Maybe he had, but she knew better than most that there were almost always two sides to any story. Her dad was never given the opportunity to tell his version. She decided to withhold the fact that even though the ceremony was cancelled he'd told her to expect him in the next few days. Hopefully between now and then she could convince her brother to at least listen to what the elder Fowler had to say.

"I just think we should give him a chance, that's all." Letting him stew on that for a while, she opened her door and changed the subject. "You ready to see what a little luck and some hard work can produce?"

That wasn't very far from the truth either. Jared had just returned from a harrowing experience where the child he never knew he'd had with Annie Campbell had been kidnapped along with another little girl. It had taken Jack and a team of Jared's old SEAL friends to save the children from a dangerous psychopath.

While Jack and Kyle—he'd insisted—continued the search for the missing suspect in her case, Ty, Jared, Mitch, and the rest of the crew had achieved miracles in the last week. They'd finished the lobby, brought in the new stage, hung the heavy velvet drapes, and laid the carpeting. All that was left to do now was bolt down the many rows of refinished chairs done in a durable corduroy material to ensure years of heavy use. The old building had now recovered much of its original grace thanks to Ty's commitment and dedication. Katy couldn't be happier.

He had gifted her with the new set of keys this afternoon after confirming that she didn't plan on going there on her own. He said he had to attend some mysterious meeting out of town and wouldn't be back until late. When Katy tried to wrangle the details from him, he'd just grinned and told her she'd have to wait and see. So she decided it would be a good time to show Kyle the changes. This was their heritage, something that shared a special place in both their minds. She hoped he would be pleased with the results.

Katy led the way to the new reinforced steel doors that Ty insisted upon. He was determined the security on the building would be top-notch. Jared had installed a new high-tech video surveillance system with cell phone access so that they would always be able to catch the feed. And sensors were rigged in strategic locations so that if tripped a silent alarm went straight to the sheriff's office. When Katy questioned Ty on the need for such an elaborate system he pointed out that it was better to be safe instead of sorry, especially after the craft store break-in and the assault from a few days ago.

She opened the door, searched for the lights, then hurried amid warning peeps to the security box and keyed in the code, relieved when silence ensued. It would've been somewhat embarrassing to have the police race over to investigate if she'd gotten it wrong. She turned to smile at Kyle and noticed his widened eyes as he took in the improvements. Warm pride and tenderness flooded her heart for the man who had remodeled the theatre the same way he'd rebuilt their love.

Katy set her purse down on the admission counter and wandered over to her brother. "So, what do you think?"

Kyle looked at her with suspiciously bright eyes, which caused her own to well up. "I think if the rest of the joint looks this good you've found a keeper."

She let out a startled laugh. "That sounds a little chauvinistic. Just because a man can hunt or build doesn't automatically make him the breadwinner, you know."

He shook his head as though in sympathy for mankind. "Poor Ty. I hope he realizes what a pain in the butt he's saddling himself with." Then he chuckled and ducked Katy's punch.

"Hey, you're supposed to be on my side," she joked.

He quit laughing and stared at her with eyes as clover green as her own. "I am, Katy-bug. Always."

Katy choked up and leaned forward to give her brother a swift hug before turning away to give them both time to regain their composure. She cleared her throat and pointed to the entry. "Let's go see how much is done inside. Ty was telling me about the stage he designed. I can't wait to see it in use."

As she strode toward the theatre doors, her brother at her side, Katy thanked God for bringing her back to Ty and this second chance at a closer relationship with her brother. Funny to think if not for her marriage plans, none of this might ever have happened.

A lingering sadness at the loss of Doc Johnson, whose funeral they'd attended yesterday, lingered. The townspeople had filled the church, anxious to say their farewells to the much-loved man. He would be dearly missed in the community. And if her heart panged for a lost opportunity to bring their son to this loving environment, she tried to set it aside.

"Okay, wow, color me impressed." Kyle murmured, as he followed her into the main auditorium.

Even though the lighting was muted due to the missing chandelier, it was obvious Ty had pushed his crew hard to accomplish what he had.

"I know, right?" Katy swung her arms out wide to encompass the room. "Can't you just see it? Every row filled with laughing, carefree faces all brought together by a children's play or maybe a long awaited movie." She danced a few steps down the aisle, her feet silent on the plush carpeting. "It's almost like we're kids again, isn't it?" She turned in time to catch a reminiscent smile tilting Kyle's lips as he watched her silly antics.

"Looking at you right now, yes. I remember how much you loved trailing Dad up and down the rows. I think you liked catching teenagers in trouble," he teased.

"I did not," she protested, then grinned. "Okay, maybe I did. Just a little. It was fun watching them scramble to get their feet down. Or couples racing to straighten clothes before Dad's flashlight caught them in the act." Which is how she met Ty for the first time.

Katy turned and wandered down the rows of loosely placed seats while Kyle took a shortcut and went to check out the stage area. Halfway down she stopped and backed up a couple of rows. This was it, she was almost sure. The place where the warm amber glow from her father's flashlight had first landed on the lanky blond with his arms wrapped around a scantily dressed girl. At first the younger Katy was scandalized, then amused as they scrambled to cover up what they had been doing. But then the teen had turned his laser blue eyes on her and she was captivated.

Trailing her fingers over the bumpy texture of the cranberry colored corduroy covering the back of the seats, Katy admitted that was the moment she began the road to womanhood. Oh, she'd had crushes and was into puberty with all the drama that entailed, but Ty made her want... more.

Suddenly her cut-off jeans and cute tops weren't good enough, she'd needed clothes that would better highlight her budding form. The long, fly-away hair that she barely brushed half the time, had to have a new, more flattering style, even if it took twice as long to maintain. The worn sneakers gave way to toe-pinching heels that made her coltish legs seem longer.

And then came the stalking.

Katy dropped the folding seat and flopped into the chair, her gaze turned inward as she remembered the embarrassing few months spent chasing Ty wherever he went. Now that she thought about it, she was lucky he hadn't reported her. Then, just when she was about to give up hope of ever being noticed, it happened.

He'd gone to the Soda Shoppe with a bunch of his friends after school and she'd coerced Rebecca into going with her. They'd sat at opposite ends of the restaurant but it didn't matter, she could still gaze at him like a lovesick puppy all she wanted.

Katy had turned sixteen the month before and desperation was making her brave. She was the only one out of their group who hadn't had a boyfriend yet. She didn't want just any guy though, she wanted Ty.

"This is crazy, he doesn't even see you," Rebecca whined. She was an introvert and hated going into crowded spaces.

She was right. He hadn't made eye contact with Katy since that moment in the theatre. Maybe it was time to let him go. Find someone who actually appreciated her efforts to change into something more than the tomboy she'd always been happy with before.

"Okay, let me go to the washroom and then we'll leave." Katy promised, her heart leaden. She rose from the bistro chair and weaved through the crowd, head kept low past Ty's table, and down the short corridor to the bathrooms.

But when she stepped out a few moments later, it was to find Ty leaning against the wall across from the door. Her heart immediately began to pound like a racehorse entering the backstretch.

Not sure how to react, Katy stuck her chin in the air and looked down her nose at him. "You waiting to use the girls? 'Cus I gotta tell you, it'll be a while."

In response he crossed his leather clad arms over his chest and smiled.

Ty Garrett just smiled at me. If she wasn't so busy trying to look cool, Katy would've fainted right then and there.

"I see you haven't lost your attitude," he said.

And that's when she knew. He hadn't forgotten her either. The pseudo image faltered and she backed into the closed door behind her. It was one thing to chase after a fantasy, but another to face reality. She was nothing more than a kid with a crush. He was way out of her league and he knew it, she could see it in those Paul Walker eyes of his.

Katy didn't know what to do with the feelings he evoked. Her skin seemed more sensitive, alive with the forbidden urge to touch and be touched. He'd gone a bit heavy on a popular aftershave her brother favored, but Kyle had never smelled this good. Maybe she was hallucinating.

"Cat got your tongue?" he teased, and tipped his head to one side as though trying to figure her out.

Ha, good luck with that. She had filled journals trying to do the same thing. Embarrassment turned her ears and cheeks a fiery pink. It made her defensive.

"What do you want?"

He slowly straightened and the hallway shrunk. "Maybe I thought it was time we quit playing this game."

Oh, great. He knew she'd been following him and was warning her off. Okay, it was no more than she deserved. Time to find Rachel and go home to lick her wounds.

"Look, I'm sorry. It won't happen again. I gotta go." Except when she pushed away from the door he didn't move, and suddenly there they were, practically chest to cheek. Katy froze. She couldn't have moved right then if someone yelled fire.

His lean fingers slid along her jaw and her body broke out in prickles everywhere. *Oh, boy.* He tipped her head up until she had no choice but to show him her humiliation.

"I think you misunderstood. Let's start again. We've never been formally introduced. Hi, I'm Ty Garrett, and you are?"

Wishing I was invisible.

Katy took a step back and thrust out her hand. "Katy. Katy Fowler." He took her hand and solemnly shook, a motion belied by the twinkle in his eye. Whatever, she was so over him. Pulling free, she wiped her now sweaty hand on the seat of her pants and started to edge along the wall, ready to make good on her escape.

"I think we should go out," he said abruptly, stopping her in her tracks.

If this was a joke, it was in very poor taste. "I thought you said we should quit playing." Katy tried, but she couldn't interpret the almost pained look that flashed across his face.

"Trust me, this doesn't feel like a game," he said. "Maybe I was just waiting for you to grow up."

A small explosion jerked Katy up in her seat. What the...? She stared in stunned horror as one of the Grecian vases, which had always stood like sentries on the second floor railing, disintegrated before her eyes. The chunks of cement flew in all directions like deadly projectiles.

Kyle.

Where was her brother?

She was on her feet and dashing down the aisle before the dust cleared. Her heart in her throat she desperately scanned the stage area where she'd last seen him. Something was wrong, he would be checking on her if he wasn't hurt.

"Kyle," she cried, panic setting in.

A faint moan led her to the far wall. "Kyle, say something. Please."

Tripping over fallen debris, she hurried to her brother's side. Pieces of concrete and part of the railing covered the top half of his body. Katy grabbed the wood and hefted it aside before gently brushing the mortar away. Blood oozed sluggishly from a wound on his temple. She ripped off her sweater and bunched it up before pressing against the cut. He flinched. That was hopefully a good sign, at least he felt the pain. Head wounds were notorious for heavy bleeding. Katy was more worried about where he'd actually been hit. An injury to the temple could cause death.

He may have sustained an epidural hematoma where there is often bleeding of the tissue between the brain and the skull bone and not easily detected. She needed to call an ambulance but didn't want to leave him alone. Why did she have to go and leave her purse in the entry?

Katy's fingers trembled as she set them against his clammy skin. His pulse was thready. There was no choice, she had to go.

Then she heard a noise behind her that turned her blood to ice.

"Hello, bitch. I told you I'd be back."

CHAPTER TWENTY-ONE

Ty watched over the loaders as they carefully placed the crate in the back of his truck. He closed the tailgate and turned to thank the store manager for doing such a good job of lightening his bank account. "I hope you feel bad about this, you old codger."

The man just smiled, well aware he'd made a good sale today. "Come on now, Mr. Garrett. A purchase such as this is an investment in the future."

"Whose? Your grandchildren?" Ty shook his head and climbed into the cab. He started the motor and with a wave out the window, drove toward the highway home. It had taken longer than he wanted but it would be worth it in the end. He couldn't wait to see Katy's face when she saw it hanging in the theatre. He'd had to drive damn near to Canada before he found a dealer carrying the right merchandise.

She'd be disappointed; Ty had promised he would be back tonight. That wasn't going to happen now. Even if he drove straight through it would take three hours to get there. At least she'd given up the hotel room at his insistence. If it were his choice she'd be in his bed, but since her brother was staying with them they'd decided on her having the room down the hall that she'd occupied before. For now.

That hadn't stopped him from some late night rendezvous however. It was actually fun tiptoeing around in his own house in order to get some booty. Ty grinned. He could just hear what Katy would say if she heard him call their lovemaking a booty call. He couldn't wait to get home and see her again. It had only been a few hours and already he missed her.

Ty had tried dating over the years. He'd even come close to love a couple of times. There was a woman last fall he'd dated and thought that she could be the one, but then an old friend of Jared's came to town and stole her away. In the end it wouldn't have mattered anyway. As soon as Katy came back he knew there was no one else. They'd wasted so many years apart. But, no more.

He still had the ring he'd bought her in high school and planned on placing it upon her finger when he returned. It wasn't near as fancy as the rock Katy's ex had weighed her down with, but that was okay. He'd scrimped and saved as a teen because he'd chosen it as a gift of his love, and there was no price tag you could place on that. When he was closer to home, he'd give Jared a call and have him take Kyle out for a night on the town. Maybe stop at the store for some strawberries and champagne. Ty grinned. He would never have taken himself for a romantic, but he certainly was when it came to Katy.

He almost missed the warning chirp from his phone. He turned down the music and listened, but there were no incoming calls. Ty shrugged off the foreboding feeling twisting his gut in knots and lowered the window, whistling. He drove another ten miles before it dawned on him what that beep might mean. Jared's new security system.

His hands tightened on the wheel and his foot pressed down on the gas pedal. He kept an anxious eye on the road until he found a place to pull over. Signaling, Ty turned in and slid to a dust raising halt.

He grabbed his cell from the console and started thumbing, in search of the app that would connect him with the theatre's new camera system. Why hadn't he paid more attention when Jared walked him through everything after the install? He jabbed the little icon and waited for the application to load.

C'mon, c'mon already.

Shit, he only had one bar. Ty hopped out of the cab of the truck and using his arm like an antenna, wandered around the side of the road looking like an idiot. Suddenly the picture came in and what he saw stopped him in his tracks.

Kyle, at least it looked like Kyle—kind of hard to tell with the whole *Carrie* thing going on—was wandering dazed among chunks of what seemed to be cement shards all over the floor of the main gallery. His hair was matted with blood and grotesque rivulets ran down his face.

"Kyle, what the hell happened?" Ty roared. Where was Katy? Fuck, he knew he shouldn't have left town. "Kyle." No response. Obviously the audio feed was down.

Ty jogged back to his pickup and gunned her back onto the road with chirping wheels and irate honks from fellow travellers. Shit, he was too far away to do any good. Hopefully, the motion detectors had done their job and set off an alarm for the police.

Using hands-free, Ty called Jared.

"Yeah, I see it," were his friend's opening words.

"What the fuck happened?" Ty was beyond frustrated. His foot pressed the pedal to the medal and the scenery became nothing more than a blur.

"I don't know, man. Everything was fine when I locked up last night."

Ty had given the men a much-needed weekend off after all the hard effort they'd put in, now he wished he hadn't. "I have no sound on my end, how about yours?"

He was desperate to learn of Katy's whereabouts. She must have decided to show off the theatre to her brother. There was no way she'd leave his side if he were injured.

Unless she had no choice.

"Me either. Some… knocked the wiring out or the cops would already be there." Jared's words came through the truck's radio disjointed as Ty moved in and out of range.

"Call now. I'm on the way." Ty swallowed hard. "Make sure she's all right."

"Will do. Don't worry, she's probably looking for the first aid kit, you know Katy."

Ty hung up. He sure as hell hoped that's what was happening, but the twinge in his gut had turned into a stabbing pain.

Katy couldn't believe this was happening. Her brother lay unconscious at her feet with a possibly severe head wound and a mad man stood behind her with a gun pointed at her back. Talk about your crazy melodramas, if this was on stage it would be a hit.

She rose slowly and turned to face her nemesis, keeping her body between him and Kyle. "What do you want? My purse is on the counter up front, take it and go." The man wore a balaclava but the eyes were the same. It was the shooter from the alley, she was sure of it.

He laughed, and the spooky sound filtered by the cloth raised the hair on her arms. "You think you can get rid of me that easily? Oh no, I've been thinking about this day for a while now." His thumb caressed the stalk of the gun and made her want to throw up. "You and me, we're going to have us a little fun and maybe if you ask me nice, I might let that brother of yours live."

Katy gulped down her panic, aware that if she let him see how scared she was he'd use it against her like the rabid dog that he was. "Look, my family has money. Let me make a call and I can get you whatever you want. But, you have to get help for my brother. Now."

"Tut, tut, tut. I don't think you realize who it is that's calling the shots here." He waved the gun in the air and giggled. "Get it? Shots? I crack myself up sometimes." Then in an abrupt about-face, the gun leveled out and pointed straight at Kyle's head. "Maybe you need some incentive to listen."

He cocked the weapon and Katy shrieked. "No."

She flung herself over her brother's prone body, the tears she'd held back pouring down her face. "Please," she cried. "I'll do whatever you want, just leave him be. Please." She wasn't above begging if it meant her brother might live. This was a nightmare. Where were the police? The security system should have sent out a silent alarm by now. Kyle needed medical aide soon. She had to find a way for him to get the help he needed. Whatever the cost.

"Get up." And when she didn't move fast enough to suit him, he grabbed her by a handful of hair and screamed, "I said, get up."

Forced to awkwardly climb to her feet, Katy barely held back the cry of pain. Her hands went to the hair caught in his grip and held on, trying to ease his hold. Good thing she had a tough scalp. Her abductor yanked on the swathe of hair in his hand like a set of reins.

"Let's go."

They tripped through the debris-laden aisle, his elbow pushing her where he wanted her to go. When they arrived at the foot of the stairs heading up to the second level he stopped her.

"Wait a minute."

In the next instant her arm was wrenched behind her back and a plastic cuff went around her wrist. "Give me the other one." When both were tied together he said, "Up you go, nice and slow. Just remember which one of us has the gun and you'll be fine."

With every fiber of her being Katy prayed someone would show up to save them before it was too late. Ty would be devastated. They'd finally found each other and now this. It wasn't fair. She hadn't even told him about her efforts to find their son yet. She'd thought there would be time later, when their relationship had gained firmer ground.

As she stumbled up the dark staircase Katy focused on the past week, filled with firsts for them as a couple. The first night spent in each other's arms. The first time they made breakfast together. The first time they made love after breakfast. Their first shower together. Moments of intimacy that she wasn't ready to give up. She wanted to build a life with Ty, to have children, and grow old together. She certainly didn't intend to spend her last hours with the psycho following one step behind her. The urge to fling herself backward and knock him down the stairs was overpowering. Except that with the tight bindings on her wrists there was no way she could save her fall. It would do no good for Kyle if she broke her neck trying to be a hero.

At the top her abductor grasped her arm in a bruising grip and yanked her to an even darker corner of the room. The seats had been removed up here for refurbishing and their harsh pants echoed off the walls.

"Please," she cried. "Let me go. You don't want to do this."

Katy fancied she could hear him lick his lips. "Oh, that's where you're wrong, missy. Your momma should have never messed around with ol' Ramsey. She made promises she never bothered to keep." He mumbled something behind the mask, and then said louder,

"Besides, you and me, we gots us a score to settle. You made me kill that old coot the other day. Now the cops ain't ever going to let me alone. Someone has to pay for that."

Shocked, Katy barely even noticed when he forced her to her knees and began unscrewing a section of the floor beside them. What did he mean her mother made him promises? How did her upstanding, snobbish mother know a man like this? None of it made any sense.

He finished the last fastening and used the screwdriver to pry the floorboards up and out of the way. It revealed a hidden passageway that Katy had no idea was there. And if she hadn't known about it, chances were her brother didn't either.

"I think bootleggers made this in the old days to hide their booze. Now I get to use it to hide my floozy." He chortled. "You first, and watch out for that first stair, it's a doozy." He slapped his thigh and laughed, so cocksure of himself. "I'm full of them today."

He was full of something all right, and humor wasn't one of them. He stood back with that gun glinting at Katy like an evil eye and waited for her to climb to her feet—not easy with her hands tied behind her back. Going down those rickety stairs in the dark without overbalancing was going to take all of her iffy abilities. Time enough to figure out what was going on when she made it to the bottom all in one piece.

After being made to wait while he lowered the hatch and re-screwed it, this time from beneath the floor, Katy concentrated on placing one foot solidly in front of the other and heaved a silent sigh of relief when she came off the last stair. They'd gone round and round the zig-zag staircase until now she wasn't sure exactly where they were, but she had a feeling her time was running out.

It was probably a futile hope someone might hear her cries for help. The room he'd pushed her toward after traversing a dank tunnel filled with cobwebs and who knows what else, smelled of mildew and moist soil. The only light came from a small flashlight in Ramsey's hand. At least there was a slight stream of fresh air coming from beneath a wooden door. Her heart jumped in anticipation of escape.

He noticed where she was looking and chuckled, the sick bastard. "So you want to leave me already, do you? Now what would be the fun in that?"

He set the flashlight on the floor and pulled the balaclava up and over his head. Katy shuddered as his features came into view, casting a huge shadow on the wall behind him. He looked so... average. Like the guy next door, or the clerk who bags groceries. The kind of person you'd pass on the street and never even see. Nondescript brown hair, brown eyes, even brows. All of it so normal.

Yet inside resided a monster.

And he wanted her.

CHAPTER TWENTY-TWO

Ty broke the sound barrier in his race to return home. If any cops wanted to give chase, good. The more, the merrier. Jared had called back with regular updates, none of them satisfactory.

"You better pull over for a minute," he warned.

"What's going on?"

Jared hesitated, then flatly stated the words Ty had been afraid of hearing. "She's missing."

Ty's heart clenched. He jerked the wheel, and the tires squealed as he fought to regain control. "What the hell do you mean, missing?"

"We've scoured the building, man, she's not there."

"What the fuck's going on, Jared?" Frustration was eating him alive. He hated the fact that he wasn't there. Stupid shit ran through his brain like a sieve. She'd changed her mind and skipped town. Her ex had come and spirited her away. She'd decided she needed more time. None of which explained what happened to Kyle or the falling vase.

"Calm down, you won't do her any good if you're dead." Before a fresh wave of panic could hit, Jared relayed the facts. "I called Jack who phoned for backup. We got there about the same time. He'd already checked the station and there were no reports of the alarm going off."

"So, Kyle had Katy's key. That's no reason for an alarm, right?" Then Ty picked up on what hadn't been said. "Are you saying the accident wasn't a coincidence?"

There was a moment of heavy silence. "No. I'm sorry, man. I wish I had better news. Someone infiltrated the theatre and sabotaged the motion detectors and audio. We were just lucky he missed that camera I put in the speaker box."

"Who? Who did this?" The memories of Katy's earlier assault flashed through his mind. "Oh shit, no. Please don't tell me it's her attacker." But inside he knew. Fate had stepped in and thrown them another curveball. Son. Of. A. Bitch.

"The camera caught him hiding behind the curtain on stage. He must have been watching them the whole time. He wore a balaclava, but it's him, we're sure of it. As soon as they separated he moved in. We've replayed the tape a few times now and I noticed him pull something out of his pocket. I thought it was a cell phone, but now I'm figuring it for a detonator.

"As soon as Kyle got close enough the bastard tripped the switch and the vase on the second floor railing exploded." Jared's voice portrayed his grim anger.

Ty punched the steering wheel. He couldn't fucking believe this. "What about Katy? Was she hurt?"

"No, she was across the room when it happened. Listen, you're not going to like this," Jared warned, as if Ty had liked anything about this situation so far. "As soon as she rushed over to help Kyle, the asshole jumped her. He held a gun on them. It was obvious either she left with him or he was going to shoot her brother."

Ty pushed the guilt and terror he felt to the back of his mind for now. If ... no, *when* he got her back, he'd spend the rest of his days showing how sorry he was that he hadn't trusted her. Here she was fighting for her life and he'd been worrying about his own pansy-assed feelings of abandonment.

He rubbed a shaking hand across his mouth and sucked in a harsh breath before replying. "Okay, I'm about two hours out. Keep looking, man. She's... everything. I can't lose her again, Jare. I just can't."

"I know, bro, I know. Jack has half the damn town out searching. We won't quit until we get her home. You just drive safe, we'll handle this end." He hesitated a moment, then said, "I got your back, buddy. I won't let anything happen to your girl."

Ty swallowed hard around the lump in his throat. "Thanks man, I know you do. See you in a few." He clicked off before he started blubbering like a baby.

The thought of what that animal could be doing to her right now was enough make his blood run cold, so he cranked up the tunes, opened the windows for the bracing night air, and drove like his life depended on it.

Because it did.

Katy kept a wary eye on her abductor as he went to the door, cracked it open a couple of inches, and checked the area. It was full on night now. Unless she did something to notify someone of her predicament soon, this was going to be too late.

Heart in her throat, she gathered her courage and rushed toward him with her head down like a battering ram, screaming at the top of her lungs. She'd hoped to catch him off guard and maybe smash his hand in the doorjamb so that with any luck he'd drop his weapon, but that didn't happen. As soon as she opened her mouth he slammed the door shut and turned so that she literally fell into his arms.

"Shut up," he hissed. His hand, the one with the freaking gun, came up and covered her mouth with bruising force. Then he laughed, his eyes in the dark two glowing embers of spite and malice.

"You're a spry one. We're going to have a good time together, we are. Ol' Ramsey likes teaching lessons to smartass women who think they're too good for the likes of me."

He rubbed his disgusting crotch against her belly. Her eyes widened in terror and her heart beat like a frightened bird against her ribcage. Her legs buckled. If he hadn't been holding her she would have collapsed to the ground. The smell of his garlic laden breath made her gag and he threw her away from him. She fell, injuring her back against some crates and bruising her side, then sank to the ground hard. Her shoulder blades screeched with pain from the strained position she had them in. She couldn't even feel her fingers any more.

The only thing she had left to protect herself with was words. Maybe if she could distract him for long enough and someone, *please God*, heard her scream, help would come. If not... that didn't bear thinking about, so she rushed into speech.

"Why are you doing this? Who are you?" And the question she most wanted answered, "How do you know my mother?"

"Nosy little thing, ain't ya?" He paced the narrow confines of the room like a caged animal, kicking up little clouds of dust in his wake. Katy choked and realized they had to be in some sort of storm cellar. Crazy to think her and Kyle had run over every inch of the theatre as children and never noticed that passageway.

"Your darling momma hired me to cause a little mischief for her ex by sabotaging the renovations. You just happen to be my bonus." His smarmy gaze trailed across her sprawled form. Katy hurried to tuck her legs into her chest.

"Your mom figured she could order me around like one of her minions, but I don't take commands very well. We'll see who's bossing who by the time I get done with you."

He was stark raving crazy.

But at the same time a grain of truth ran through his bluster. Katy had known for some time now that her mother was growing unstable. At first it was little things, like forgetting names and whether or not she had milk at home, when in fact there would be quart after quart sitting in the fridge going bad. Then the extreme mood swings began; from amusement to condescension, to anger and confusion. It wore on everyone around her. Soon the board members were asking Katy if something was wrong and all she could do was shrug it off. If not for the years of service her mother had given to the hospital, they probably would have relieved her of her duties.

To carry a grudge like the one Ramsey suggested her mother had done for ten long years was almost beyond comprehension. Katy understood how the sting of her father's betrayal and the humiliation of being the one left behind had worn on her mom's psyche. But to hire a thug to destroy something which had meant so much to all of them... that hurt.

"You'll never get away with this. Let me go, and I'll make sure they know you didn't hurt me," Katy pleaded.

He stopped at her feet, a tall menacing silhouette in the darkness. "Yeah, let me think that over."

He swooped down and smacked tape over her mouth. "No."

"Quiet now, I need to think." His finger traced a snaky line down from her cheek to the top of her breasts and Katy reared back and screamed, though the sound was no more than a muffled moan.

"C'mon now, is that any way to treat a future lover? I've seen how you rub all over that idiot contractor. Wait until you have a real man between your legs, then you'll purr for sure." He snickered and his teeth gleamed like those of a cobra.

He stood and moved to the other side of the room for a moment, returning with a length of rope in his hand. Katy thought he meant to kill her right then and closed her eyes to picture Ty. She had no wish for a murderer's face to be the last thing she remembered. Instead, he reached behind her, hooked the rope around her cuffs, and then tied her to the crates.

"I have to go see a man about a car," he said. "You stay here and be a good girl while I'm gone. I left you enough rope to stretch your legs, don't make me regret it."

He waited patiently for her agreeing nod. Then he rose, taking the flashlight with him, and made his way to the door. Katy watched in nervous anticipation. She hoped the police had somehow been notified and were even now awaiting their chance to capture her assailant. But no, he slipped through the door without any sound at all.

The ominous clicking of a lock and the near pitch-blackness set her teeth to chattering and a cold sweat formed all over her body. She counted down the minutes until she thought he was gone, desperate to move, but not enough to get shot.

Or worse.

The thought of his hands on her body roiled in her stomach. She wanted Ty and the safety of his strong arms. Yet at the same time she was fiercely glad he was nowhere near. It was bad enough her brother lay injured because of this madman. If he were to hurt Ty she couldn't live with herself. Especially since it was due to her screwed up family Ramsey was in Tidal Falls at all.

Determination stiffened her backbone. Katy had never been a quitter and now was certainly not the time to give up without a fight. So even though every muscle in her body cried for rest, she pushed herself to her feet and tested the limits of her prison. The rope stopped about her body length from the door. So close. She gritted her teeth and dug in her heels, but the crates wouldn't budge. Panic began to set in and she had to force herself to calm down. Think. Breathing from the narrow slit he'd left on her nose was difficult enough without adding hyperventilating to her list of problems.

Something scurried across the floor on the other side of the room and Katy shivered. She didn't mind mice as long as they kept their distance, rats on the other hand... not so much. What she wouldn't give to have Ty's cat here right now. The humorous picture of a tiny kitten going up against a rat king, and winning, lightened some of the tension from her shoulders.

First thing she needed to do was figure out a way to cut the plastic cuff around her wrists so that she could untie the rope. Katy shuffled her way back to the crates and turned her back so she could search for a way in with her bound hands. Whatever was in there weighed a ton, so hopefully it could help her achieve her goal of escape. They were wooden, rough in texture. A splinter caught under her nail and she winced, but didn't give up.

Finally, in the farthest corner, Katy felt something give way beneath her questing fingers. Adrenaline rushed through her system and gave her the necessary strength to ignore the tight binding digging into her wrists and grab the edge of the board. She yanked for all she was worth. At first nothing happened, but then with a squeal of old nails releasing their hold, the wood slowly gave way. Katy fell to her knees and grunted against the pain. She hung her head and sucked in great gasps of air into her starved lungs before rising.

Her questing hands found the hole she'd made in the box and gingerly moved inside, not sure what to expect. When she came up against the smooth touch of cool glass she thanked her lucky stars. Wine bottles. That explained the passageway. If these were bottles from the prohibition era they could be valuable. Unfortunately she needed to break one. Katy grasped the neck and through sheer perseverance managed to pull it free of the crate. Her fingers, slippery now from blood, lost their grip and the bottle crashed to the floor and smashed over the top her shoes.

Now came the fun part, dropping onto her knees in the dark without cutting herself from the glass. The pungent aroma of fermented fruit and yeast was enough to knock her socks off. She edged away from the smell first and then attempted to ease down to the floor, but in actuality flopped onto her side more like a beached whale. She lay there for a moment trying to recover, her cheek in the dirt and frustrated tears sliding down her dirty face, and then inch-wormed her way backward until her hands felt the first pieces. The thought of angling a sharp shard of glass anywhere near her wrist was daunting but she had no choice, it was the only option.

She searched for a chunk that wasn't too long and unwieldy, ignoring the little pricks to her fingertips. When she had one that felt like it might work she twisted it upward and carefully sawed back and forth between her wrists. It was painstaking work and she kept shooting anxious glances at the door, realizing she was running on borrowed time. Finally, one end let go, and then the other.

She was *free*.

But, oh, the pain. Her arms, loosened from their enforced captivity, were swarmed by what felt like hundreds of bees. The pins and needles brought fresh tears rushing to the surface, and it was a good thing her mouth was still taped because she would most certainly have cried out her agony.

It took a few moments before Katy could move enough to work the knot in the rope. Good thing she had a brother in the army who insisted on sharing his knowledge. This time it was invaluable. As soon as she broke loose of that restraint, Katy grabbed the edge of the tape, and before she could second-guess herself, she ripped.

Ouch.

Sore fingers reached up and touched tender lips. After this was over she was booking a spa day.

Now to figure a way out.

CHAPTER TWENTY-THREE

Ty roared into town and drove straight toward the theatre. He could already see the rotating red and blue lights from a block away and started to shake. If anything had happened to Katy his life wouldn't be worth living. He'd already wasted so much time on foolish pride.

"Please don't let it be too late," he whispered, and prayed someone was listening.

Jared's truck sat kitty corner across the boulevard with its lights shining into the trees, the driver's door wide open and the engine still running. Men in uniform swarmed the area like ants, some on the grounds, while others streamed in and out of the building. An ambulance and two fire trucks stood to the side, ready to take on casualties, while a yellow tape held a group of curious onlookers back. It was like a scene from a crime thriller, except this was all too real.

Ty threw his gear shifter into park, opened the door, and ran. Except then there were hands holding him back, ripping at his clothes and yelling his name. Someone tackled him from behind and sent Ty crashing to his knees.

He roared his agony, sure that it was over. He was too late.

She was gone.

"Ty, it's me. C'mon, Ty, settle down. It's Jared, buddy. I'm here. I'm here." The voice kept repeating in his ear until he came back into his body and realized he lay face down on the ground with arms pinned behind his back. Someone—Jared—lay over top of him, crushing Ty with his weight, but he didn't care. It didn't matter, nothing mattered. Tears dripped down his face and wet the sidewalk under his cheek. The pain was indescribable. Almost as though someone had reached in, squeezed his heart, and then ripped it from his chest. Maybe he was dying. The thought gave him hope. He'd follow Katy any way he could—even into death—without regret.

"Ty, c'mon man, Katy needs you. Don't do this to yourself." Jared's words were slow to penetrate, but when they finally got through Ty jerked, scraping his chin in the process. The sting sobered him up.

"Katy needs you." Jared's words reverberated in his head.

She's alive. Desolation turned to hope.

Despair became anticipation.

He struggled to rise, filled with renewed strength. Desperate now to know where she was, and to verify for himself that she lived. "Let me up," he rasped.

"I will, but first you have to promise to listen." Jared applied just enough pressure on Ty's back to hold him in place. "You ready?"

Anyone else and he would have come up swinging, but Ty knew his friend was just trying to help. "Yeah, I'm good." Jared released his grip and both men rolled to their feet, chests heaving.

"Where is she, Jare?" Ty looked toward the ambulance but the doors were closed. When there was no immediate answer he swung an anxious gaze at the theatre where two men guarded the door.

"He still has her, doesn't he?" It all made sense now, the amount of officers still on scene, the emergency vehicles, the air of expectancy everyone wore like a shield of armor.

Jared released a heavy sigh and ran a hand through his hair. "Yeah, he does. They're treating Kyle right now. He has a concussion and some lacerations, but otherwise he's going to be okay. Jack questioned him, but never got much. The vase knocked him out and he doesn't remember anything before it happened."

"I need to get in there, see it for myself. You coming?" Ty was already in motion, taking the stairs up to the front door of the theatre in a controlled rush. He waved the guards impatiently out of his way, even as Jared cleared it from behind him.

"He's with me, let him go." Jared ordered. Then in an aside, "Of course I'm coming. How else am I going to keep you out of trouble?"

If this wasn't so serious, Ty would have smiled at that. He'd lost track of the number of times he had to pull Jared's ass out of the fire before he got burnt. The guy was a walking trouble magnet, but there was no better person to have watching your back and Ty knew it.

"Where did Jack get all the extra help, the National Guard?" He hadn't seen so many different uniforms in… well, ever.

Jared caught up to him in the main entry. Men and women with white booties on their feet combed the area, some taking pictures, some with fingerprint kits making a mess of his new floor and walls. As if that mattered. Strange, the weird paths your mind takes to deal with shock.

"Funny guy. I phoned the chief and he called in some favors. We *will* get her back, Ty. I promised."

Ty nodded, overwhelmed by the support. Jared had some friends in high places from his SEAL days, but this was something else. He clapped a grateful hand on

Jared's back. "Thanks, man. I don't know how I'll ever repay you, but thanks."

"Just name your first kid after me," he joked. "Unless it's a girl. Actually how do you feel about Geraldine?" Then he dropped the jokes and pointed to the admission counter against the far wall. "I found her purse there, untouched. Her cell phone was inside, so no tracing her that way."

"Shit." Did she leave the purse behind, or had her assailant? "What do we have on this guy?"

"I think I'll let Jack share that news." Jared nodded toward the gallery. "He's in there, talking to Kyle and manning the search teams."

Swallowing around the ball of anxiety threatening to escape, Ty strode toward the entry. Maybe once he had a better idea of who he was up against, he could form a plan of action. Right now it felt like he was wading in quicksand—and going down fast.

The gallery was a zoo. Like the front entry, men and women were combing the site of the explosion and the surrounding area. There were people searching the stage and the second floor galleries. Another group squatted in front of a guy sitting on a chair near the front, a pack—no doubt filled with ice—held to the back of his head. Kyle.

Long strides carried him swiftly to Katy's brother. Filled with a sudden rage he made no effort to control, Ty reached through the throng, latched onto Kyle's shirt, and heaved the injured man out of his seat. He pulled back his other arm, ready to drive the asshole in the face, but the watery, defeated eyes staring back at him were Katy's. Silence reigned throughout the room as he stared into the battered face. His arm slowly dropped to his side. It was obvious Kyle was taking this every bit as hard as he was, harder even.

"Go ahead, hit me. It's what I deserve." He lowered his head and Ty could see the gash seeping along his hairline. "I let her down. Some protector." Bitterness coated his voice and turned it sour.

The anger faded, leaving compassion in its wake. Ty tugged the younger man into an awkward hug. "It wasn't your fault. Pull yourself together. We need you." With a final slap on the back, he released him and turned to the others. "So, where is she?"

Jack threw the pen he'd been holding down on the blueprint he'd been crouched over on the floor. "This is your baby, you tell me." He frowned in frustration. "We've been over every square inch of this place with a fine tooth comb, and got nothing. The cameras from across the street show the two of them entering after your crew vacated for the night," he nodded at Kyle, "but no one left. The back door is still locked with a steel bar across it on the inside. I have to admit I'm baffled."

He sat down and leaned back on his arms, stretching his legs in front of him with a tired grimace. "I'm getting too old for this shit."

The others got back to work as Kyle, Jared, and Ty circled the papers on the floor. On closer inspection Ty noticed the discolored parchment of what looked to be the original plans for the building.

"Where did you find that?" He bent down to get a better look.

"Kyle called his father who had it in a safety deposit box here in town. He called the bank manager and approved its release."

Ty glanced at Kyle. That had to be one tough phone call. Katy had mentioned the rift between father and son. The first conversation in years and it was to share grief. Knowing Kyle wouldn't want his sympathy, Ty turned his focus on the older plans. Where the copy he'd been given for the restoration showed the extensive updates to the building's structure, this one displayed a much different picture.

The original building, once a narrow three story hotel, had sat squarely in the middle of the town lot. He noticed the square footage now was easily double that amount, filling the space outside from front to back. Obviously, when modernizing the previous owners decided to build a shell around the exterior instead of ripping it all apart.

Something bothered him, but he couldn't quite... *wait*. Ty checked again and sure enough, the interior dimensions were still the same.

"Well, I'll be damned."

The other three looked up inquiringly.

"What?" Jared and Kyle asked at the same time.

"Kyle, did your dad ever mention any hidden rooms, or flights of stairs?" Ty took the new copy Jack was looking at and placed it over top of the old one. Then he held the two of them over his head. The light streaming through the paper highlighted the different dimensions of the building, past and present. An air of expectancy took hold of the men. Ty hoped he was on to something here.

"Shit, would you look at that?" From Jared.

"Son-of-a-bitch," Jack swore.

"No, not that I remember," Kyle said, clearly surprised at the variations between the two prints. "Look." He pointed to the faint outline of a second set of stairs. "There's only one flight up to the gallery. Where did that one go?"

As one they all rose and rushed for the stairs leading up to the second floor where the vase had fallen. Ty reached the top first, having taken the stairs three at a time, and startled a couple of officers taking snapshots of the explosion site. Their hands went straight to their firearms before they saw Jack following close behind, and relaxed.

"Search the walls," Ty ordered. "Every square inch if we have to." They fanned out and began a light tap-

tapping in a crisscross pattern, searching for a hollow square that would prove Ty's theory. He worried that the noise would alert Katy's abductor, but there wasn't time to carefully remove each panel until they found what they were looking for. The closer he came to Kyle working the next section of wall, the more desperate he became.

C'mon, it has to be here.

But it wasn't.

They each went over their sectors a second, more thorough, time with the same depressing results. How could he have got this so wrong?

Kyle slid to the floor with a muffled thump, banging his head against the wall in defeat. "I can feel her fear, it's driving me crazy, but at least I know she's alive." The "*for now,*" went without saying.

Jared had cocked his head and was listening, his brow furrowed. "Do that again," he said, staring at Kyle.

"Do what?"

"The wall, behind your head. Hit it again," Jared's voice was a mixture of impatience and excitement.

Kyle looked at him like he had a screw loose, but turned and complied by smacking the area with the palm of his hand. There was a hollow sound but when he moved a few inches and did it again the thud of a beam could plainly be heard.

"See? Nothing." Disgusted, he flopped down and that's when they all identified it; the floor. It wasn't in the walls, it was under the floor. There was a mad scramble to grab some lights and rip back the carpeting. Sure enough, a hatch was revealed, sealed shut with four-inch screws all around the perimeter. Frustrated, Ty called for a drill and began the painstaking process of removing each one until finally, they could lift the cover. Jack drew his weapon. Jared and Kyle manned the flashlights.

And Ty held his breath.

Katy thought she heard a faint noise and paused in her frantic search for another way out of her dank cell. She'd hurt her shoulder already throwing herself against the outer door in the futile hope of either breaking the lock or the hinges, but both were in better repair than she'd hoped. Now she was feeling her way around the room, careful to avoid the broken bottle. The door that they'd entered through had to be here somewhere, but she couldn't locate it in the dark. And the walls were gross. Moist from the dirt and spongy with mildew, she hated to think what kind of creatures occupied the space with her.

She'd just started again, her poor cut fingers stinging on the wood, when the muffled sound of tires on gravel warned her that her time was up. It was him, Ramsey. She'd taken too long to free herself and then lay the trap. If only she had moved faster she could have been gone when he came back. Instead, now she was going to have to corner the tiger in his den.

And hope she survived.

Katy hurried over to where she'd strung the rope, and picked up one of the unopened bottles of wine she'd stashed there just as the scrape of a key in the lock came from the other side of the door. Holding the end of the rope and the bottle like a Louisville slugger, Katy waited for the door to open, her heart in a flat-out run of the bases.

One. *Shit.*

Two. *Crap.*

Three. *Dammit.*

The door swung open letting in a blast of cool air. A second later the dark shadow of a gun and the hand holding it appeared in the opening.

A little more, just a little bit farther, come on.

Her inner chant paid off. He stepped right into the circle of rope. Katy pulled for all she was worth. His feet came out from under him. He went down hard on his back, and the gun discharged into the air.

She flinched, and then with a triumphant shout, brought the bottle over her head and slammed it into his upraised arm with enough force to knock the gun flying. He shrieked in pain and anger. That was all the incentive she needed to get the hell out of there. Except he was sprawled out in the doorway.

Now what?

She swooped low, grabbed up another bottle, shook it, and then popped the cork. The pressurized liquor spewed from the top and coated his face, burning his eyes with the acidity. He screamed, his fingers clawing at the liquid.

Katy wasted no time. Inching past his legs, she was almost to his shoulders when he realized what she was doing and made a grab for her ankles. She went down with a startled cry, to land across his chest.

She pummeled his neck and shoulders. It did no good. He rolled and the next thing she knew, she was under him with her hands pinned to the ground.

Strike.

CHAPTER TWENTY-FOUR

Ty lifted the cover on the hatch. It revealed a wooden flight of stairs leading down into what seemed like the depths of Hell. An inky darkness ate up the flashlight's meagre beam. The men covered their noses as the scent of decades worth of secrets drifted out of the hole.

"That's nasty. It smells like your last girlfriend, Kyle," Jared smirked.

"Fuck you," Kyle mumbled from behind his hand.

"Okay, quiet you two. We don't want to tip this guy off if we can help it," Jack warned. "I'll lead. Keep those flashlights covered with something. We only want enough light to see, not to announce ourselves."

Ty stayed silent. His body vibrated with the urge to race down those stairs and save his woman. They were close, he knew it, but Jack was right. Too much noise and they'd only make things worse. Jared muted his light by stuffing it under his shirt, Kyle followed suit, and then they were on the move. Thank Christ.

It was slow going. They had to carefully check each tread for creaks, and for safety's sake. The pitch darkness came from the fact that the short flights doubled back on each other, like a fire escape. Probably exactly what this had been, back in the days of the hotel.

They were on the third set of stairs when the unmistakable blast of a gunshot ripped Ty's heart from his chest.

No.

He was on the move before the reverberations ended, shoving his way past Jack and ignoring his call to wait. He braced his hands on either side of the wall and jumped, taking a leap of faith. Landing, he turned and did the same with the next flight, and the next, the men behind following like a herd of buffalo now that the need for silence was past.

At the bottom there was a narrow tunnel of a hallway leading toward what he assumed was the back of the building. He trotted along the corridor, slashing his arm at the cobwebs stretching out to grasp at his hair. The men followed him, the rays from their flashlights making eerie shadows on the walls. Muffled cries came from beyond an old wooden door at the far end. His foot went up and slammed the thing open. It banged against the inner wall and startled the two people on the floor.

The figure on top threw themselves to the side and the one on the ground sat up and screamed, "Ty."

Katy, dear God. Ty raced forward, only to get knocked off his feet by the man on the floor. He landed hard on his back, the wind temporarily knocked out of his chest. He blinked and sat up, and then froze. The son-of-a-bitch had a gun trained on Katy who was highlighted by the peek-a-boo moon as she sat in the open doorway.

"Don't move," Ramsey growled. "And you two," he waved at Jared and Jack, "over there, where I can see you."

His face was grotesque under the flashlight's beam. Some kind of red liquid, too thin for blood, had made channels under his eyes and down the sides of his nose.

A weird, fruity smell fought with the dank odor of a root cellar, permeating the room.

"Throw down your weapon," he ordered Jack. "And you, drop the flashlight." He motioned toward a tensed Jared. At Ty's slight nod they slowly let their weapons drop, hands away from their sides.

Ramsey laughed and used the gun to point at a softly crying Katy. "You got a live one there, don't ya? Me and her, we've been having a good time together. Haven't we, *bitch*?"

Ty swore and lunged forward, only to come to a sliding halt when the unmistakable click of a cocking chamber could be heard throughout the room.

"You think I'm fucking around here?" The humor was gone, replaced by an almost frightening calm. "One more move and her head is going to explode like a watermelon." His red-rimmed eyes tracked the men. "Try me."

With his attention split in so many directions, Ramsey had missed seeing Kyle creep into the room. Ty tried to give Katy's brother time by keeping the focus on him. "What do you want? How did you find this place?"

Ramsey smiled. "That's right, you haven't heard. Me and that one's ma," He nodded at Katy, "we go back a ways. She's the one that set this all up, you know."

Kyle froze. Ty silently urged him to not make any dumb mistakes. He was Katy's only hope at the moment.

He tried to keep Ramsey talking, "Why would she do that? She loves her daughter."

"Yeah, well, not enough to keep her away while she got me to destroy her husband's pet project." His teeth gleamed in the dark. "She's the one that told me about this room. Said it would make it easy to slip in and out of the theatre so's I could destroy all that hard work you was doin'. The girl there," he lifted his chin in her direction. "I decided, she's my bonus. What do you think? Should be a good ride, eh?"

Ty saw red. He flew through the air. An animalistic roar of rage erupted from his chest as he plowed into the bastard's smarmy face. Out of the corner of his eye he saw Kyle dive for his sister as the gun exploded, searing his side. But there was no stopping him now. The fear of the past few hours rose up and drove his fists to smash down over and over, until there was nothing but a bloody pulp beneath them.

Finally, the crazed haze cleared. He gave in to Jack and Jared's pleas, rolling away and gasping for air. As soon as he could move again, he sat up and looked over to the doorway.

Kyle crouched over his sister's still body, tears streaming down his face.

Katy was dreaming. She had to be. In this imaginary world she floated weightless among the clouds, held safe in Ty's warm embrace. Their son, with his father's bright mop of curls and shiny blue eyes, chased butterflies in a never-ending meadow, while her dad and brother lounged side by side in the thick green grass. They laughed and chatted around a picnic lunch spread out on a red checked cloth, completely at ease in each other's company.

A noise in the distance caught their attention, and a dark cloud suddenly loomed on the horizon. The breeze picked up, flirting with the edges of the gingham fabric. Kyle stood and yelled something, though she could hear no words. Her dad rose also, slower and stiffer, and raised a hand over his head, his expression worried.

Katy shifted, unaccountably upset. Then Ty's hand captured hers, his lips grazed her cheek, and she settled once more.

Down below, Kyle and her dad were searching the meadow. The sun disappeared and the wind had whipped the trees into a frenzy. Something was wrong. Katy's brow furrowed. Where had the trees come from? They were great, hulking giants, casting gloomy shadows upon the forest floor. She didn't remember a forest being here. Where was... funny, why couldn't she remember his name? She should know his name.

Her heartbeat picked up on her agitation and answered with a rhythmic pounding of its own. That sound again. Familiar, yet she couldn't quite place where she'd heard it before.

They'd reached the trees now and were fighting to breach the impenetrable vegetation. Then she saw him. He was skipping down a path straight toward two shadowy figures she couldn't make out. Katy cried out, desperate to warn her son, to slow him down until Ty could reach him.

Ty. She meant Kyle of course. Ty was here, with her. Safe.

Except it was him, and he'd managed to breach the tree-line. Thorny branches cut his face and ripped at his clothes, but he kept going, running as though something horrible was about to happen.

And then it did.

One of the shadowy figures lifted a gun, and then boom, a shot rang out and Ty dropped to the ground, unmoving. The gunman slowly stepped forward into a stream of light bursting through the trees. Katy gasped; it was her mother.

Her father's soft voice with its hint of Irish brogue summoned Katy from the depths of her dream. "C'mon, Katybug, talk to your old man. I didn't come all this way just to watch ya sleep, you know."

She moaned. Her head felt like a jackhammer was going off inside of it, and her mouth tasted as if she'd swallowed a jar of cotton balls, both dry and scratchy.

Her eyelids were glued down and she had to force them to open. Blinking, Katy realized what that noise was she'd been hearing in her dream; a heart monitor. She was in a hospital.

As her vision cleared, she made out the shape of her brother and her father sitting by her side, a green curtain at their back separating them from the next bed. They looked tired; their eyes puffy and bloodshot. As soon as Kyle noticed she was awake, he rose and leaned over the bed, tears flooding his sea green eyes, so like her own.

"Thank God, you scared the living shit out of me. Don't ever do that again." He kissed her cheek and gave her a careful hug before standing up and clearing his throat. "I need a coffee now that you're back among the living. Anyone else?"

"Yeah, I'll join you." Katy's dad leaned over and kissed her, "I love you." He smiled into her blurry eyes, then rose and shared a look with someone on her right side.

"Nah, I'm good," the voice murmured.

She turned her head and there he was. The light above her bed shone down on his beloved face and she could see his scrapes and a big bruise darkening his cheek. Ty lifted the hand he'd been holding and brought it to his lips.

His eyes, filled with love, crinkled at the corners as he smiled. "Hi, Sleeping Beauty."

Her insides turned to goo at his reference. God, she loved this man. More than she'd thought possible. When he'd taken that bullet...

"You were shot." Her voice was so raspy she doubted he understood. But then he grinned and lifted his T-shirt to show off a shiny white bandage wrapped around his ribs.

"You mean this little thing? It's just a graze, nothing to worry about." Then he sobered. "Nothing like you.

Shit, Katy, when I looked over and saw you laying there... you scared the bejesus out of me."

"What happened?" she mumbled, her words slurry.

He reached over and brought a cup with a straw to her lips. "Here, drink this."

The fresh coolness of the water was a balm to her parched throat. She took a good drink and then sank back into her pillows, flinching a little at the persistent throbbing in her head and shoulder.

Katy cleared her throat and tried again, "Was I hit?"

Ty ran slightly shaky fingers through the hair at her temple. "Yeah, you were caught by a ricochet. It grazed your shoulder. Then when you fell, you hit your head on the door-jam. Swear to God, I lost ten years of my life when I saw you laying there."

They stared into each other's eyes and acknowledged they were lucky to be alive. It could have turned out so much worse.

"Mom...?" Katy asked, half afraid of the answer.

Her dad leaned forward and grasped her hand. "We're getting her some help. The doctors think she has early stage dementia, so the judge is willing to make some concessions. She'll have to get counseling, of course, but we're hopeful that she can avoid jail time."

Katy nodded, saddened that she hadn't picked up on the symptoms herself. Maybe if she had...

"What about Ramsey?" she whispered, and a shiver skated up her spine.

Ty answered that one. "You don't have to worry about ever seeing that asshole again. He's going to be spending the rest of his days avoiding picking up the soap in the prison showers, and I for one, couldn't be happier."

Ty's gaze dropped to her mouth. Katy licked her lips. That was all the invitation he needed. He leaned toward her. And held out a small blue box. A ring box.

She lifted her head and met his wobbly smile.

"Will you marry me?" His voice had deepened and his hand shook as he opened the case and lifted out the diamond ring. "I know it's not much, and if you don't like it, I can buy you another."

Tears dripped off her chin. Overwhelmed, Katy held up her left hand and nodded. Ty slipped the ring on and she twisted it in the light, delighted with the simple design.

"It's perfect. I love it." Joy warmed her entire soul. She loved this man more than she'd ever thought possible and now they were going to build a life together.

"I will love you for all our lives," she promised.

"Forever," he vowed.

EPILOGUE

Katy stood in the lobby of the theatre, her heart beating with nervous anticipation. The counters gleamed with a fresh coat of polish while tall urns of oriental lilies, matsumoto asters, roses, and pink peonies, accented with stems of variegated ivy filled the room with a heavenly scent. In the gallery friends and family waited expectantly under the glittering dome of the five tier chandelier Ty had given her as a wedding gift. Any sign of the lunatic who had tried to destroy their lives, long gone.

The piano rang out with rolling notes of faith and devotion. She trembled. It was time.

Sara Reed's daughter, Jessica, led the way in a dainty pink dress with Annie's son Christopher clutching the ring pillow in both hands and marching alongside in a little tuxedo that brought tears to the women's eyes. Rebecca glanced back to give her a quick thumbs up before she too, began her march. Then Sara and Annie went next, in a swirl of sea foam green dresses.

"Ready?" Her father stood beside her, elegant in a navy suit and crisp white shirt. A hint of tears moistened the corners of his eyes, darkened with emotion. "I'm so proud of you, my girl."

The bouquet of lush white peonies and garden roses rattled in her hands. Her smile came out wobbly and she had to blink back her own tears to avoid ruining her makeup. "I love you, Daddy."

"Oh, Katy. I love you, child." He hugged her tight, then bent his arm and held it out to her in a grand gesture. "Let's go meet that soon-to-be-husband of yours, shall we?"

Butterflies danced in the pit of her stomach. Soon. Soon she would be Mrs. Katy Garrett. Images of the two of them as teens floated through her mind. The time Ty had taken her for a date to the park. He'd pushed her on the swings and then they'd goofed off on the teeter-totter. After a while they'd taken a walk through the grounds. He'd stopped by a tree marked by hundreds of initials.

"Know what this is?" he'd teased, and caged her body with his to the trunk.

Of course she knew. Everyone talked about the kissing tree at school, but this was the first time she'd been here with a boy.

"Why don't you tell me?" she'd tipped her head back, closed her lids, and pursed her lips like she'd seen other girls practice in the mirror. When nothing happened, Katy opened her eyes. Ty hadn't moved. His gaze, focused on her mouth, made her stomach feel funny. Squishy. Embarrassed, she went to slip under his arm braced on the trunk near her head.

"Don't," he whispered.

She froze.

"You're so damn pretty," he said, half under his breath. Then he leaned forward and their lips met, and Katy just knew.

T. G. + K. F. forever.

He'd carved a heart in the bark right where their first kiss took place and signed it.

It had taken time to heal the wounds of the past but as her father gently guided her down the aisle toward her groom, Katy rejoiced. Grateful that fate had guided her steps to the man who was meant to be her destiny.

The theatre was filled to overflowing, everyone dressed in their Sunday finest. The women dabbing their eyes with tissue while smiles of joy spread across their faces. The men fiddling with ties and too-tight jacket buttons, waiting patiently for the wedding to end so the dinner could begin.

The aisle lay covered in delicate white rose petals that floated around their feet with every step, releasing more of their heavenly scent. The room was aglow with ethereal light coming from the hundreds of tapered candles situated on pedestals among the lavish flower displays. Sweet Essence, the local flower shop, had done an outstanding job on making Katy's vision a reality. It was just as she'd always dreamed, right down to the hero.

Her first glimpse of Ty about took her breath away. He stood at the front of the stage near the stairs, Jack, Jared, and Kyle at his side. Tall and almost unbearably handsome, his classic black tux fit him like a glove and highlighted his gorgeous blue eyes.

Those eyes, so serious and full of love, guided Katy the last few steps to the stairs. As the ritual passing of hand from father to husband took place and she climbed toward her future, Katy knew the best was yet to come.

Reviews are the lifeblood of any successful author. Without you, we can't be heard.

If you enjoy the story, please consider sharing on your favorite social media sites, as well as GoodReads and from wherever you've bought the book.

Thank you,

Jacquie Biggar
Jacquiebiggar.com

OTHER BOOKS BY THIS AUTHOR

Tidal Falls: Book #1 in The Wounded hearts Series

Nick Kelley spent the last few years of his life working as a dog handler in the U.S. Marine Corps. His sole focus was to keep his team alive in the midst of chaos. When he fails to notice an IED in time and loses most of his teammates, Nick shuts down. It takes meeting and falling in love with a woman in danger to make him realize life's worth living.

http://jacquiebiggar.com

Subscribe to My mailing list to find out first about upcoming releases, contests, recipes, and more. http://eepurl.com/2MFvX

OTHER BOOKS BY THIS AUTHOR

The Rebel's Redemption

Annie Campbell has a good life for her and her young son in the mountain town of Tidal Falls. She's dating the sheriff, owns a successful business, and has the support of the community.

So why isn't it quite enough?

Jared Martin left Tidal Falls a hotheaded youth, and now, after eight years in the military, he returns a bitter, disillusioned man.

Then he finds out he's a father.

When an old enemy follows and causes mayhem in the small town, can Jared overcome the odds to protect the woman he's always loved and the child he never knew, or will it be too late?

http://amzn.to/1CSFJQH

NOTE FROM AUTHOR

I thought I'd share with you the beginning of my love affair with writing.

Normally, procrastination is my enemy. I like to get done whatever it is, as soon as I can, so that I don't have to worry about it any more.

In school I worked hard to stay in the top ten every year. So when I came down sick with the measles and missed two weeks of grade nine, I was devastated. How was I ever going to catch up? I had less than a week to write a compelling story for Language Arts or get a failing mark.

Angry and frustrated, I sat in our living room, pen and paper in hand, staring at a bright yellow bouquet of cheerful looking daffodils. I wanted to hurl them across the room. It wasn't fair. Why was I being punished for getting sick?

But then an idea popped into my head. A silly, farcical story. If the teacher wanted an essay, fine, I'd give him one. And so, Count Daffodil, was born. After the first paragraph the words flowed quicker, I could see the scene in my head and needed to get it down on paper. (Sound familiar?) I spent the rest of the day writing, and by the end of the night I had my story.

The next day I turned it in and immediately felt ill all over again. It was dumb. The teacher was going to hate it. I'd be a laughing stock. Funny how easy you can build something up to catastrophic proportions when you lack self-confidence.

We had to wait two weeks for the results. I was on tenterhooks the entire time. Sure that my mom would blow a gasket because I'd goofed instead of giving it my best shot.

Then came the big day.

I was scared to look. Finally, I couldn't take it anymore and turned to the last page. These were my teacher's words:

I'm glad I didn't read this at night. It's been a while since I was so enthralled with a story. Very professionally done. The suspense, the ending, the style was excellent. I think I'll read it to the other classes. Very impressive.

Not only did he read it to the other grade nines, he read it over the intercom to the entire school!

Because of Mr. Thomas and a hapless bouquet of sunny daffodils, a writer was born.

Jacquie's first book, Tidal Falls, a romantic suspense novel about second chances, released September of 2014.

~  *Jacquie Biggar*

ABOUT THE AUTHOR

Jacquie lives in paradise along the west coast of Canada with her husband, daughter, & grandson. Loves reading, writing, and flower gardening. She spoils her German Shepherd, Annie, and Calico cat, Harley. And can't function without coffee.

Learn about upcoming news, contests, recipes, and more from my newsletter.

You can follow me on:
http://jacquiebiggar.com
http://Facebook.com/jacqbiggar
http://Twitter.com/jacqbiggar

SIGN UP FOR MY NEWSLETTER: http://eepurl.com/2MFvX

On the next page you'll find information about my other books.

Thank you for letting my story into your world for a few hours.

Best Wishes,
Jacquie